GOING OFF THE RAILS

GOING OFF THE RAILS

(The Madness of John Biddle)

Keith Mapp

Book Guild Publishing

Sussex, England

First published in Great Britain in 2010 by
The Book Guild Ltd
Pavilion View
19 New Road
Brighton, BN1 1UF

Typeset in Baskerville by
Ellipsis Books Limited, Glasgow

Printed in Great Britain by
CPI Antony Rowe

A catalogue record for this book is available from
The British Library.

ISBN 978 1 84624 453 7

The Commuters' Lament

The come and the go, the ebb and the flow,
The crash of the slamming of doors,
Then the pounding of feet over platform and street,
Up the stairs and across office floors,
And we'll stay here all day for the pittance they'll pay,
In the thrall of the bosses, the corporate whores,
But we'll do as they say 'til the end of the day,
When the trains from the station will take us away,
From a place that we hate, where we stay working late;
But tomorrow we'll come back again;
Tomorrow we'll come back again;
Each tomorrow we come back again.

Ivor G Rudge
From The Poetry of the Working Classes

This book is dedicated to all of those who have suffered in the past, to those who suffer now and to those who will suffer in the future. If Confucius had been alive now, he would have warned us all that the light at the end of the tunnel is either a train coming the other way, or some sod with a torch bringing us more work to do.

1

Week One: Day One – On a Tuesday

John Biddle, forty-five years old, actuarial technician by profession and serial under-achiever by nature, looked up from the pages of the cheap paperback novel he was reading as the brakes were applied and the train he was travelling on began to slow down, preparing to come to its half-expected, or was it almost-inevitable, stop. He stared out of the window to see how far down the line they had got, knowing that, once again, he was going to be late home from work.

With a screeching squeal of tortured metal from the brakes and wheels, the train jerked and shuddered to a halt. The braking system, its job done for the time being, released some of its pent-up compressed air, with what sounded to John like a resigned sigh, as did most of his fellow passengers, or 'customers' as they were now habitually referred to by the train operating company in whom they invested so much of their money and so much of their faith; then an expectant silence descended over them all. Somewhere, some way distant from where John was sitting, a compressor clattered into life, rebuilding the air pressure that had been lost as a consequence of the train's sigh, with a series of staccato reports reminiscent of the sound of a far-off machine-gun being fired. Slowly, silently, a shiny new air-conditioned train slid into position alongside its geriatric, traditionally-ventilated, slam-door cousin and stopped, on what was, somewhat laughably just then, called the fast line.

On board John's living relic from a bygone era of railway history, everyone waited expectantly. They were not disappointed for very long as, after a short pause, preceded by a rich assortment of crackles and clicks, a disembodied, metallic voice with a harsh Mancunian drawl issued from the loudspeakers in the carriage ceilings. It was the sort of voice made popular by television interviews with certain pop stars and footballers, and regarded by some members of the younger generations as being 'cool'; not that John, being no longer a member of any of those generations, really understood what being 'cool' entailed.

'Good evening,' it said, displaying no irony in its tone, 'this is a customer announcement.'

Please note that we're being referred to as customers yet again, thought John, and not the passengers we used to be and all thought we still were.

'This is your En-Route Customer Service Director speaking,' the voice continued.

The guard, thought John.

'I've been informed by Central Train Despatch that we're being held here on a red signal due to a suspected fatality ahead of us at High Weald International Airport Station, our next station-stop on this service, which will serve to delay us on our journey southwards from London tonight. As I currently have no information on the expected duration of this ongoing delay, I don't know how long we'll be stopped here; it depends on how serious the incident is, but I hope we'll be on the move again shortly. As soon as I hear anything, you'll all be the first to know. In the meantime, I'd like to take this opportunity to apologise on behalf of South Coast Regional Trains for this current and ongoing delay and for any inconvenience this may cause to you on your onward journey this evening. Thank you.'

Click. Over and out. For a short period of time nothing

happened, then, in a scene that John knew without needing to look was being repeated along the length of both stationary trains, the man sitting opposite him reached into the inside pocket of his suit jacket and pulled out a mobile phone. Although John knew little about new technology, and would hardly have been able to distinguish a Blueberry from a Blacktooth, nor have been able to tell you clearly what the purpose of either of them was, he was able to identify this phone from its TV advertising as one of the latest models modern communications technology was able to provide: compact, slim-line, flip-topped, full colour-screened and internet-enabled; but with just one purpose to fulfil: to prove to the observer that its user was important enough, or self-important enough, to posses it. What happened next was boringly, depressingly, predictable, as the man flipped open its top, stabbed out the digits of someone's phone number with his stubby, be-ringed fingers, held the device up to his ear, then waited briefly while it connected, rang, and was answered.

'Hello, it's me,' he announced loudly. 'I'm on a train.'

I'm on a train, John groaned inwardly. Is that what it's all come to? Untold centuries of intellectual development; generations of organised education and schooling in English language and literature; billions of pounds, dollars and yen of investment lavished on the inventions of some of the brightest minds the world has been able to summon up, and what's the result? The opportunity for a substantial proportion of the population to make contact with another substantial proportion, simply in order to tell them, in prose of such inventive power, wit and imagination that it would have the likes of Shakespeare and Dickens spinning in their graves, that they were, at that exact moment, precisely where they had said they were going to be – 'on a train'.

John lost interest, as the man proceeded to relate the story of the crisis so far to the listener on the other end of the line, whoever that poor person might be. He gazed idly

through one of the train's open windows at the scene outside; at the gardens and backs of the houses standing alongside the railway line, all bathed in the golden sunshine of a
gloriously warm early summer's evening. The temperature
inside the stationary train began to rise, there being not a
breath of breeze to blow in through those open windows to
balance the effect of the sun's rays beating down on the
roofs of its carriages. Soon, if they did not resume their
journey, it would be hot enough to bake bread in there. Even
the stuffed shirt opposite, with his poser's mobile phone,
would be forced to remove his jacket and loosen his fashionable, silk, designer-designed tie.

Out there, John mused, are people who are not like us;
people who are free of all this; people who, having finished
their day's work or, perhaps, not even having gone to work in
the first place, are already at home, dressed in cool and casual
clothes, sipping iced drinks, relaxing, reclining, in elegantly
comfortable chairs on patios and lawns shaded by parasols,
gazebos or striped awnings in pastel shades, made from tac-
tile materials bought at out-of-town garden centres or by mail-
order from glossy lifestyle magazines. The lucky bastards!

The fact that John was unable to see any of those 'lucky
bastards' through his open window did not, in his mind,
mean that they did not exist – just that he could not see any
of them at that moment. Even if they did not exist, his para-
noia would invent them for him: a particular brand of para-
noia that led him to believe that everyone else was doing
better, was having a better time, a better life, than he was.

John sat; the stuffed shirt sat; everyone sat; and waited:
reading, dozing, staring out of windows; secretly hoping that
the air-conditioning on the train standing on the fast line
alongside them was broken, so that they did not have to
believe that they were currently the most hard-done-by group
of people on the face of the earth; hoping their train would
move off first, so that they would not have to suffer the

torture of watching the other depart without them. They got their wish as, a short while later, with a sudden clatter and a jerk, suggesting that the driver's cab was fitted only with an on-off switch rather than a control which allowed graduated and even acceleration, it lurched back into motion and ran on smoothly, if slowly, into the station ahead.

'We have now arrived at High Weald International Airport Station,' the disembodied voice returned to announce.

Another statement of the bloody obvious, thought John. Right up there alongside 'Tomorrow's another day' and 'If that had gone in, it would have been a goal'.

Doors crashed open and slammed shut along the length of the train as people climbed in and out of it, half drowning the continuation of the guard's announcement, which none of the regular travellers on the line would have needed to hear to know that it carried on with the words: 'If you are leaving the train here please make sure for security reasons that you take all your possessions with you and keep them with you at all times while on the station or inside the airport terminal building. On leaving this station, this train will now call at Bridges Junction, then all stations to Asham.'

John looked out of the window, searching with macabre fascination for some sign of activity associated with the crisis causing the delays. There was none. Nothing but the usual crowd at that time of the day during the working week: a potentially lethal combination of sprightly commuters and business travellers weaving their way between groups of confused elderly American tourists pulling behind them wheeled suitcases the size of small wardrobes, or in some cases small rooms, vainly searching for a member of staff to confirm to them personally what they had been told by the station's public address system; not that the announcements it made were difficult to hear – they merely seemed to be in another language. One of the tangible improvements that had followed the privatisation of the railway network in the 1990s was in the quality of the public address systems and the announcements they conveyed to the travelling public. The trains were no more punctual or reliable than they had been before the sell-off, but at least now you knew the reason why – or what the people who ran them chose to tell you was the reason why. Indeed, those announcements were now so clear and effective that, when the son of a friend of John's whose house backed onto the station in the town where they lived spoke for the very first time, he recited to his stunned parents a list of all the stations between there and the coast, including those whose platforms were so short they could be served only by the first four or five coaches of the trains which stopped at them.

Beyond the crowds battling on the platforms, there was nothing to be seen, save the latest set of advertisements for the region's most popular mobile phone company, the people's service-provider of choice, Roamer-Phone. The public face of Roamer-Phone at this time was the current presenter of television's top motoring magazine programme, a hulking great brute of a man whose sheer physical bulk was exceeded in size only by his own opinion of his own opinions. His face was a hard one to avoid, as it leered down menacingly from bill-boards and posters all over that part of the rail network, mounted above or below Roamer-Phone's sound-bite of the moment: 'Going somewhere? Go roam-yer-phone.' John seriously doubted whether train travel ever featured in this man's itinerary, however. He would be more likely to be phoning his latest blonde, celebrity-wannabe girl-friend from the driving seat of his over-powered sports car saying, 'I'll be home in twenty minutes, darling; make sure there's room in your parking slot for this throbbing monster of mine!' than 'Hello, it's me; I'm on a train . . .'

As John looked out, the air-conditioned train on the fast line slid into view on a distant platform, beyond the bill-boards, and a game of chance was launched for those on board it who were headed in the same direction as he was. Both these trains, it was clear from the station announcements, would stop next at Bridges Junction, before parting company to go in different directions. John's would turn to the south-west on a branch line leading to the coast and call at all stations to Asham, while the other stayed on the main line, continuing south, running semi-fast to Bigton. This created a dilemma for those who wanted to change trains. If they got off now to sprint across the bridge to the other platform, they might be in luck and get there before the train they were aiming to catch left. But if they were not in luck and it departed while they were still running up and down stairs and avoiding bewildered Americans with super-sized luggage, the train they had just deserted might also leave before they could turn around and get back to it. Then they would be stranded. If they stayed on board in the hope their train would leave ahead of the one onto which they wanted to transfer, and thereby arrive at Bridges Junction first, allowing them the luxury of an unhurried transit from one to the other, they might behold their intended onward transport sliding quietly away from the platform at the airport, leaving the train they were on standing in its wake, and subsequently find it had left Bridges Junction before ever they arrived there. Choice, John reflected, is often one of the most stressful things the human animal can be presented with.

As it turned out, both trains left the airport station at the same time and ran on down the line into Bridges Junction almost side by side, the result of a conspiracy between their drivers and guards, John suspected, to see if they could be there for such a short space of time they could both pull out quickly enough to leave behind on the stairs or in the underpass between the platforms everyone who was trying to transfer from one to the other. Money would, he thought, change hands later, depending on the result.

On leaving Bridges Junction, John's train travelled the

short distance to its next stop, Southnewtown. Beyond Southnewtown it left behind the urban sprawl of industrial, commercial and then housing development that invariably springs
up around busy airports the world over, and headed out into
the open, green, gently-rolling Wealden countryside. Sunshine streamed in through the windows, accompanied by a
soft breeze, welcome and refreshing after the heat of the
earlier stoppage. After two more stops at two small villages
along the way, they were soon approaching Asham, John's
home town. There had been no more delays, and nothing
more had been said about the fate of those who were so
recently suspected of having been dead. The mobile phones
had all been in use again though, to give updates on progress
and expected arrival times.

As the train slowed down for its approach to Asham
station, John found himself pondering the question of what
had caused it to be delayed. What, he asked himself, was a
'suspected fatality'? Was it a person so grievously injured
that it was uncertain whether they would live or die, or was
it just a stationary railway worker, fallen asleep at his (or
her) post, and suspected, for a while at least, of having laid
down his (or her) life in the call of duty? The sudden evap-
oration of the delay and the lack of any visible sign of
unusual activity on and around the airport station made
him suspect the latter was the more likely explanation. Then
the voice of the guard cut in on his thoughts as the train
finally rolled into the station and that evening's journey came
to its end.

'We are now arriving into Asham station, where this
service will terminate. Please make sure when you leave the
train . . . blah, blah, blah. On behalf of South Coast Regional
Trains I'd like to thank you . . . blah, blah, blah, blah.'

The bland, formulaic, end-of-journey announcements
rolled over the heads of the weary travellers as they stood
up, gathered their belongings, not for security reasons as

instructed by the train operators, but because they actually wanted them, and headed for the exits.

John stepped down from the train and started up the steps to the footbridge. Ahead of him the mobile phones were out again, imparting the news of the train's arrival and the safe delivery of its precious cargoes. More fuss was now made over the arrival of a train, he thought, than he remembered being made when the first men had landed on the moon. How much less dignified it would have been, if the immortal words, 'One small step for man, one giant leap for mankind', that had echoed eerily over the radio link in the control room in Houston had been replaced by the ringing of a mobile phone, followed by a distant voice saying: 'Hello, it's me: I'm on the moon.' What other historic moments would have been demeaned by the use of the mobile phone? Prime Minister Neville Chamberlain would never have gone to Munich to confront Hitler; would never have returned with his famous piece of paper and would never have made his famous radio broadcast declaring: 'No such undertaking has been received, and consequently this country is at war with Germany.' Instead, the radio broadcast might have gone something like this: 'I told that Hitler to give us a bell but he didn't – tried to claim he had no signal or was out of credit or something – so I sent him a text saying, "Bugger you, mate; we're at war."' On the other hand there might have been benefits. Take the charge of the Light Brigade. A simple call saying, 'Hello, it's me. I'm on a hill, looking down on the battlefield. Stay put until you hear from me again, and don't go any-where near those Russian guns.' would have prevented a lot of the unpleasantness that followed.

Although he could be resistant to the adoption of new ideas, John was not completely closed to change and would do his best to adapt when he could see a benefit in doing so. He did, in fact, own a mobile phone, sometimes carried it with him, and sometimes even turned it on. He had bought it in case of emergencies, but did not subscribe to the view that minor train delays constituted on emergency. He was a man of traditional values and views; a true conservative with a small 'c', (or a Luddite, depending on your point of view). If you questioned him closely, you would find that, in his opinion, civilisation had reached its zenith in and around the home counties of England at about the same time that The Beatles were at the peak of their popularity, before they had gone off the rails and turned to all that flower-power nonsense. Moreover, it had reached those urbane and dignified heights without the dubious benefits bestowed upon it by any of the so-called advances in technology that had appeared since that time, of which the mobile phone was just one example; he attributed a large part of the decay in morals and behaviour to the widespread availability of such things. However, at the time he now held up as representing the zenith of all things, he had been only six or seven years old and could not, therefore, have known what adult life was really like then. He could be said to exemplify the oft-repeated remark that 'if you can remember the sixties, you weren't there'.

After a short walk, John arrived home, a two-up, two-down Victorian workman's terraced cottage where he had lived for the past twenty years, alone. He had never married or co-habited, and never felt the need to take in friends or lodgers to supplement his income. Closing the door, he put down his worn leather briefcase, hung up his jacket on the hall-stand, pulled off and rolled up his tie and put it in one of the outside jacket pockets, then walked through the dining room into the kitchen, where he took out of the fridge the single-portion ready-meal he had moved there from his freezer the night before. He quickly read the instructions, took off as much of the outer packaging as they told him to and put it in his microwave oven to cook. Here were two examples of modern technology of which he thoroughly approved: convenience food and the means by which it could be rapidly heated – and with no messy pots and pans to wash up afterwards. And if he ate it straight from the tray it had been bought in, which he often did, there was almost no washing up to be done at all. How could such life-improving, labour-saving developments not be welcomed!

Taking his meal with him when it was cooked, he went into his small sitting room and, as was his custom, sat down in front of the television to watch the early evening news. Other people got their news by reading the papers on the train, either the morning papers, or the evening paper, or both. John escaped into novels when he was travelling, preferring the more easily-absorbed presentation of the TV news bulletin to keep him in touch with daily events. So every evening, when he got in, he sat down to watch it. Later, when he was amply rested, watered and fed, he would go upstairs to shower and change his clothes ready to go out, but before he did so, there was one more part of his daily ritual to perform. After taking his tray back out to the kitchen and making himself a cup of tea, he sat down at his dining table, reached out and pulled towards him an exercise book, of the type used by school children in their classrooms, in which he kept neatly-written records of his train journeys. This he did purely for his own amusement. From time to time, usually on a weekend when he had nothing more important to do, he would get one of these books out of the drawer of his sideboard, where he kept them when they were full up, and read again the details of his regular journeys and the reasons the guards and station announcers gave as to why the trains took so much longer to get to their destinations than they should have done.

When he left the house that evening, he went to the Oxford Arms, which stood on the corner opposite the back entrance of the station. It was a pub with something of a split personality, having two distinctly different bars, one either side of its entrance. To the left it was a traditional pub: dark, heavy furniture and fittings: wooden panelling: bar; serving real ale, pork scratchings, darts, dominoes, smoking, football, and mainly blokes. On the other it was fitted out as a trendy wine bar: light wood floor and bar top, matching high round tables on single chrome columns, surrounded by high-backed chairs with steel frames. Its clientele, a generally young and well-dressed mixture of both sexes, chatted vivaciously, drank wine voraciously and refrained from smoking, for the benefit of their health and that of their fellow drinkers. It had no television, but music of the easy-listening kind played discreetly in the background. John pushed open the outside door and walked in, turning left into the gloomy warmth of the more traditional bar, where he knew he would find his friends waiting for him.

These were people he had known for many years, some from his school days, others from the early years at work. Amazingly, they had all stayed in contact as their lives slid past, and now met up regularly, usually once every couple of weeks, in a pub somewhere, to drink, chat and enjoy each others' company. Occasionally they would do something more adventurous, like take a long walk in the countryside to a different pub followed by a longer walk back – or so it seemed after their indulgence. Or they would visit the coast to enjoy the benefits of a change of air, wafting in through the open door of a seaside pub.

Amongst this group was one who regarded John as someone special, but who doubted, based on the evidence of her past experience, that he regarded her in quite the same way. She was Angela Wicks, John's first, and some would say only, girlfriend; she had been his on-off companion for years, the two of them drifting alternately together and apart in much the same way that they drifted through life, with no apparent direction or plan.

At this time they were more apart than together. Neither was anything very special, so in that respect they were probably well suited. The difference between them was that she realised this was the case; he did not, because he had never really given it any serious thought. His ideal woman was, he supposed, like most men's – a tall, blonde, rich, supermodel or actress; but he had never really gone out looking for one, perhaps because, deep down, he knew there was no point. Angela was not tall, she was not blonde, she was not rich; she worked as an accounts clerk in a local firm of estate and letting agents. John was no film star but if he had shown any sign of being prepared to settle for her, she was quite sure she could have settled for him. As it was, neither had settled for anything much at all.

Pete, sitting next to Angela, was John's best friend from school and an ex-work colleague from John's first job. He was now self-employed, doing something with computers from the workshop he had set up in the back end of his garage at home. He was a divorcee and the owner of a small, elderly, rusting, hatchback car, which John borrowed from time to time when he needed transport, as he did not have a car of his own.

Justin was another former work colleague from the early days, now a rather successful customer service manager at the airport. He was married to Sarah, his childhood sweet-heart, who sat beside him, the two of them having for once left their twin toddler daughters at home in the charge of a babysitter. This, in itself, was something of an event. Having married early, they had been confident that their fairy-tale union would soon be blessed with the children they thought would make it complete. Many years of disappointment had followed, however, without the joy of the patter of tiny feet. At last, one of the regular rounds of fertility treatment they had been forced to resort to finally proved successful, and Sarah had given birth to two tiny peas from the same pod: two little girls identical in almost every way. Now, having come to parenthood rather later in their lives than most, they were rather over-precious parents and did not get out much.

The other couple present, Mark and Christine, also had problems getting out, but for very different reasons. They had also married young but been blessed almost immediately with a child, and then again some two years later: two boys, currently a pair of teenage tearaways heading for juvenile delinquency. This made it difficult to get babysitters in the first place, and difficult for them to come out for fear of what the boys might do to any babysitter who might be duped into looking after them for the evening. That night, for the sake of their own sanity, they had found someone brave enough for the task, offered to pay them well over the going rate for the job, and escaped into the realm of a grown-up social life, a place where they were in danger of becoming strangers.

Also part of the wider group, though not present in the Oxford Arms that night, were another pair of couples, one married, the other not. These four were spending the evening together at the annual badminton championship at the sports club to which they belonged. All four were keenly competitive but worked hard not to show it. The main aim of each pair that evening, as everyone in the group knew full well, was to go further in the competition than the other two so that they could then be both modest and magnanimous about their achievement, whilst making quite sure that everyone else was fully aware that they had something to be both modest and magnanimous about. While it was true to say that they were missed, not seeing them because they were at the competition that night was generally considered rather better than seeing them on the night after it, when modesty and magnanimity were likely to be at their height on the one side, and a certain amount of bad sportsmanship and bad grace on display on the other.

Accordingly, the party gathered in the old bar in the Oxford

Arms was both smaller and happier than it might otherwise have been, and everyone there had a good time. Those who were parents talked about their children while they drank to forget them for a while. Those who were not parents listened and nodded in all the right places while not really identifying at all with what was being said. The mothers continued to talk while the others wandered off to play darts and pool, and the evening slipped away; the daylight faded slowly into dusk, then to darkness.

At just after eleven o'clock they spilled out of the pub to make their way home, all in good spirits, buoyed up by each other's company and the drinks they had downed in the course of the evening. They were the sort of people on whom alcohol had a beneficial and mellowing effect. They said a hushed goodnight to one another, respecting the right to peace and quiet of the pub's neighbours who, like them, probably had to get up and go to work in the morning, then went their separate ways.

The night was warm, quiet and still. As John walked he was aware of the sound of his footfalls on the pavement echoing off the fronts of the buildings on either side of him. Behind him, from the back station entrance, he heard a train arrive.

'Asham Station. This is Asham Station. The train now standing on platform four terminates here: all change please. All change please on platform four.'

As he reached his front door and turned the key, John had a vision of its passengers climbing the steps onto the footbridge, mobile phones clamped to the sides of their heads, announcing to friends and loved ones that the battle was over for another day, that they had been delivered safely to the station and were heading home to welcoming arms and bosoms. Wondering briefly what it might be like to be so welcomed, he went inside, closed the door behind him and headed up the stairs to get ready for bed on his own, as usual.

2

Week One: Day Two – On a Wednesday

Day dawned early across the empty countryside of southern England in that balmy summer, as the sun peeped above the horizon and began its steady climb into the heavens. The clear skies had allowed the temperature to dip somewhat overnight and left just a hint of mist hanging in the air around Bridges Junction station and the windows of its signalbox control room, standing alongside the southern end of the platform on the fast down-line that pointed the way towards Bigton and the coast.

The first train of the day was yet to pass by those windows, but behind them there was already activity. Inside that control room men and women who in the past would have been known as signalmen, regardless of their gender, would later direct and control the movement of all trains running into and out of the part of the rail network over which they had command. Inside that control room an age-old ritual was about to be played out. In the centre of the room was a table, topped by a wooden-framed, glass-panelled cover, under which there lay an open book – a large, heavy, leather-bound book, with pages made from a paper of some weight and quality, on which there was writing, in ink, in a copperplate hand. This the railwaymen knew of as 'The Book of Reason', as it contained within its covers a list of all the reasons why trains had been, and might be, delayed on their journeys along the rails of the network during the course of the day. To the travelling public, such a book, had they known of its existence, might well have been labelled 'The Great Book of Excuses', for much the same reason. Those who had compiled it had begun their work in the earliest days of the railways in the area, when steam was king and provided all of the motive power for the trains; the task of updating it had been carried on by those who had succeeded them. There, in that process of updating, lay two distinct features of the book which anyone looking at it for the first time might have found more than a little odd. The first was that, after a period of chronologically-sequenced entries during the early years, subsequent entries appeared to have been made randomly, dotted about here and there through its pages, often with large empty spaces between them. The second was that many entries – mainly, it appeared, the older ones – had been crossed through in red ink, as though they were no longer of interest. The latest batch of entries, inscribed on its pages in the freshest-looking ink, related to the operation – or, to be more correct, the failure to operate properly – of the latest generation of trains introduced on the network, the fleet of computer-controlled, sliding-door stock that was gradually replacing the old slam-door carriages. These new entries were concerned principally with computer failures, and a whole new language relating to hardware, software, modems and interfaces had been introduced.

Footsteps sounded on the staircase leading to the control room from the floor below. The door swung open to admit a group of people who entered in single file and gathered in a loose circle around the display case. These were the great and good of the several railway companies who worked at, or whose trains passed through, Bridges Junction: managers of various levels, all in freshly-washed and pressed uniforms, as prescribed for the ritual that was to follow. Once they were arranged in their places, all facing towards the table and the book, the youngest amongst them stepped forward, removed the glass-sided cover and set it aside. Then, with great care and reverence, he lifted up the book in white-gloved hands and closed it. Holding it out in front of him, its embossed leather spine facing the floor, he turned to one of the others, the one whose turn it was on that day to re-open it. With eyes closed and breath held, the chosen one ran his thumbs over the outside edges of the pages, then pushed them inside at the place he had randomly selected. The youngest member let the book fall open on his out-stretched hands and peered down at the two pages in front of him, silently counting the number of entries he could see there.

'A number between one and seven, if you please,' he said quietly to the member who had chosen, and who still stood before him with eyes closed.

'Five,' said the chooser after a short silence, during the course of which nothing moved and no sound was to be heard.

The youngest member turned away and laid the open book back on its bed of plush green baize. He placed a thin, flat piece of light-coloured wood, rather like a school ruler with no markings, below the fifth entry, as though to under-line it, turned, lifted the cover and repositioned it on the table. Then he stepped back, lightly pressing a small switch on the side of the table as he did so. Overhead, a spotlight came on, illuminating the display case, the book, the open pages and the underlined entry on them, clearly visible for the rest of the day and the night that would follow.

As we have seen, John Biddle was a man of regular habits. Saturdays, Sundays and work days each had their own sep-arate rituals and procedures to be followed. Today, being a work day, saw him awake and out of bed, showered, dressed, fed, watered and standing in his customary position on

Asham station's platform two at precisely 7:58, in readiness to join the 8:02 train from Smalltown-on-Sea to London.

John checked the time on his watch, unnecessarily he knew, as it was always set at the right time – checked each morning against the seven o'clock time signal on Radio Four while he was eating his breakfast – then looked up at the familiar script on the destination board above his head. The top line announced the impending arrival of the train for which he was waiting: Next train 08:02; Destination London River Crossing; Expected 08:02. Underneath, moving text scrolled across the board from right to left: Calling at:- Smallholt, Morlands, Southnewtown, Bridges Junction, South Suburbia and London River Crossing.

As he contemplated the board, the station's public address system burst into life, the soft, computerised, female voice it used announcing: 'The next train to arrive at platform two will be the 08:02 South Coast Regional Trains service to London River Crossing, calling at . . .', then listing all the stations whose names had just been displayed. He turned and looked south, down the line beyond the end of the platform, expecting at any moment to see the train round the bend at the end of the long straight and begin to make its approach to the station. Nothing happened. Above his head the PA system announced: 'The train now approaching platform two is . . .' and repeated the rest of the earlier announcement. Still there was nothing to be seen on the track. Another minute or so passed before his thoughts were invaded once more.

'The train now standing at platform two is the 08:02 South Coast Regional Trains service to London River Crossing, calling at . . .'

No it isn't, thought John indignantly, as though the computer that made the announcements would be able to hear him and would then correct itself. What right have they got to make such outrageous claims when the thing is quite obviously nowhere in sight?

'Please stand clear of the closing doors of the train now standing at platform two: this train is ready to leave.'

No it isn't! It hasn't even arrived yet!

It was about ten minutes later that the train finally rounded the bend and made its way along the straight, slowing down and easing gently into position alongside the platform edge. With a quiet hiss of compressed air its doors slid open. John looked up as he stepped over the threshold. The destination board was blank, this train, as far as it was concerned, having departed on its journey northwards, on schedule, some time before.

A short while later, perched no more than semi-comfortably on a seat that felt as though it was constructed from a fabric-covered plank, he thought he had worked out what might have happened. As part of the process of privatisation, the national railway network had been split up, broken down into a series of separate companies that ran its various components. The track was owned and run by one company; the trains were owned and run by others: South Coast Regional Trains (SCoRT for short) on this part of the network, Middle and East Wealden Train Operators (referring to itself as MEWTO) in the area that lay to the east. John knew that train operators were subject to fines if their trains ran late or were cancelled. These were levied by the government's rail regulator, OFFTOSS (the Office of Train Operating Service and Standards), and could be passed on to the owners of the track if the delays could be attributed to them.

What, he thought, if the right to make the announcements had also been sold off to another company, and made subject to the same performance requirements and sanctions for the delivery of poor service – something called the 'Announcements Agency', for example? That would serve to explain how and why the announcements were still made in accordance with the timetables, even when the trains were running late. John smiled with amusement at the absurdity of such a thought. His happy reverie was interrupted by an announcement from the train's automatic address system.

'This is the South Coast Regional Trains service to London River Crossing, calling at Smallholt, Morlands, Southnewtown, Bridges Junction and South Suburbia. This service is running approximately eleven minutes late due to a badger on the line at Howard's Heath.'

No sooner had that announcement ended than the loudspeakers burst into life once more. This time the voice of a real person, the guard, floated through the air.

'This is the En-Route Customer Service Director speaking. I would like to apologise for the inaccuracy of the last announcement: the delay was due to a cow on the line, not a badger as you've just been told. For some reason they don't appear to have any cows in the computer in Central Information Services, so they had to use the announcement about the badger instead. I hope this lack of accuracy has not caused you any undue inconvenience on your journey into London this morning and, once again, ask you to accept my apologies for the delay. Thank you.'

John found it hard not to laugh out loud, along with everyone else on the train, he suspected, but nobody did. They stayed silent and po-faced, as all good commuters should. The rest of the journey was uneventful, and at just after 8:55, about ten minutes later than scheduled, John's train approached the place where he would leave it.

'We are now approaching South Suburbia station, our next station-stop on this service,' the guard announced over the PA system, then trotted out all the usual messages, as per the prescribed passages in the appropriate training manual. 'Take your belongings . . . ; thank you for travelling . . . ; travel onwards in safety . . . ; mind the gap . . . ; etcetera; etcetera.'

This started with the airlines, John thought, who have such a lot to answer for. Now it's been picked up and spread like a disease – in shops; in fast-food outlets; on trains; through most parts of the service sector, in fact – by marketing men (and women) who don't seem to know any better: plastic smiles, false-sounding platitudes and cries from assistants of 'Have a nice day!' when you know full well that most of them are hoping your day will be as crappy as theirs; and all foisted on us in the place of quiet and genuine good service. And where will it all end? On the occasion of my last day on this earth, probably, with a small loudspeaker mounted in the lid of my coffin, announcing in hushed and reverential tones that 'Messrs. Diggit and Burnham (Undertakers of quality since 2003) would like to thank you for choosing to make your final journey to your burial/cremation (delete as appropriate) with our funereal service today. When leaving your life, please make sure you take none of your possessions with you as your nearest and dearest will be waiting to get their hands on them (to put them on eBay) as soon as this service is over. On behalf of our directors, Mr Diggit and Mr Burnham, I would like to wish you a speedy and safe onward journey, into whichever version of the afterlife your beliefs have led you to subscribe to. And now, as one final thought, using the words of the famous, late and much lamented Irish comedian Dave Allen, rearranged slightly to be more appropriate to the current occasion, 'May you go with *your* God.'

John stepped from the train onto the platform at South Suburbia station and made his way up the exit ramp towards the ticket barriers, still absorbed in these gloomy thoughts. On his way, he passed under the massive bulk of Overway House, the headquarters building of The Permanent Way Agency, more commonly known to the public as 'Permaway'. This was the august body which owned and operated the tracks, the signals, the power supplies and most of the stations on the railway network, and which was, in the eyes of the travelling public at least, directly responsible for a substantial proportion of the delays they were forced to endure each working day.

Overway House was a fine example of what was referred as an 'air-rights' building, a type of building constructed over the top of a number of Perma-way's stations and tracks on massive concrete columns, as a way of exploiting the value of the land they stood on and the air above them, and as a way, they claimed, of supplementing their income from tickets and keeping prices down. Cynics claimed that such schemes were dreamed up only to maximise the company's income and so please and appease its directors and shareholders. But what have cynics ever known about such things? That sentiment was, however, graphically and eloquently expressed in the alteration made by an informed and intelligent graffiti-artist to a sign John walked past twice each day, on his way to and from work. It was on the wall of the station entrance. When it was new it had read: 'This station is owned and operated by The Permanent Way Agency: keeping trains on track for the benefit of Britain'. After modification it announced that the station was being mismanaged, for the benefit of its directors.

John's place of work was in another huge, multi-storey building, one of quite a number that had sprung up in the decades following the end of the second world war, and now made the southern end of Suburbia look like a jaded off-shoot of the more affluent City of London to its north, where money for refurbishment and replacement was, apparently, more readily available. The building he worked in was the UK head office of an American insurance giant which had been expanding by buying up assets across Europe for a number of years, and had swallowed up the smaller, British company that John had worked for since he had left school.

When he started work with Gray Insurance Services, as it had been called then, their office had been in Asham town centre, not far from his parents' home. When he reached a time when he was able to buy a place of his own, it was natural that it should be located in the same town as both his work and his family; in other words, where his life had its base and foundation. But as time passed, changes were made. He continued his education at night-school and obtained the qualifications that had enabled him to take up his current post. Gray Insurance Services, being successfully run, had expanded and moved into its grand new office in South Suburbia, taking John and his job with it. John did not want to move house, so when his job relocated he joined the huge mass of people who commute to work each day, flowing in and out of our larger towns and cities like the ebb and flow of the restless, beating tide. More time passed and more changes were made. A merger with Life Insurance Services (Suburbia) added to the size of the expanding group, and when, only a few years later, the whole thing was swallowed up by the European arm of the acquisitive American company, the Phoenix Health Assurance Corporation (Europe), based in Arizona, the scene was set for the name of the whole thing to be changed to that by which it was now registered and traded in Europe: The Phace, Liss & Gray Corps. If only the person who had first thought of the name had abandoned their relentless devotion to logic for a moment and thought about what they were doing, the image of the new company might have been completely different from the one it then assumed. But whatever anyone said about the name, no-one could argue that it was anything other than entirely appropriate for a company that made most of its money from life insurance – or death insurance, as it should, perhaps more accurately, be known.

After a brisk, ten-minute walk from the station into the heart of South Suburbia, past the monstrous indoor shopping centre, past several more slab-sided, homogenous and anonymous office buildings, John reached his place of work, another rectangular leviathan which was, quite appropriately, faceless and grey, and went inside.

John's desk was in the open-plan office of the actuarial department on the twelfth floor, accessed by a lift from the lobby. This was another annoying piece of relatively new technology that not only accelerated and decelerated at a most alarming rate, but also sang out the numbers of the floors it was about to stop at and announced its direction of travel in a high-pitched mid-Atlantic voice. Fortunately, however, it stopped short of thanking its users for travelling in it, asking if they had all their possessions with them or wishing them a nice day or safe and happy onward journey.

John's view of the surrounding area from the office windows should have been a good one. It was not, because, being positioned roughly in the centre of the floor, all he could see once he was seated in his desk chair was his computer screen and the grey bulk of the mid-height fabric-covered partitions that formed the walls of his work area, or his PCC-Zee – 'Personal Corporate Contribution Zone', as it was known in his company's management-speak. Why the American 'Zee' instead of the British 'Zed'? you might ask. Was it because it was an American company and that was what they called the letter, or was it simply because it made the whole thing rhyme? No-one really knew for sure, but the chances were that it was some happy combination of the two. For a while it had been called his PCOS – 'Personally-Controlled Operations Space' – but this had been found too distressing for the surprisingly high number of young women that PLGC employed who suffered from a medical condition known as Polycystic Ovary Syndrome, which shared the same acronym. It also amply illustrated the dangers inherent in the use of abbreviations and acronyms when there are only twenty-six letters in the alphabet to choose from, and when combinations of letters used in one world can cause upset and misunderstanding if they escape into another where they mean something completely different. Indeed, not so very long ago, the chief executive officer of the American Computer Corporation, having become very concerned about the possibility of such problems arising from what he perceived as the overuse of three-letter acronyms by his company's customer-facing divisions, commissioned his main board directors to prepare a report for him on the subject, with proposals for curtailing the practice. They, missing the point of his request completely, in due course proudly presented him with the completed document, nicely bound in glossy covers and entitled 'MBR to CEO wrt tuo TLAs by ACC's CFDs'.

For those who do not already know, management-speak is a particular kind of language, or perhaps it should more correctly be termed a dialect, invented by people in a work environment who want to form themselves into exclusive groups or cliques. It is used by managers who want to talk down to the people who report to them when they have no other weapons in their intellectual armoury with which to do so because the people they manage are better-qualified, more experienced, or simply better at doing the job their department exists to do than they are. Management-speak is easily identifiable by the fact that those who use it will not be understood by the sane and rational people at whom it is directed. A user might, for example, say to a group of people: 'When I look down your pipeline I can't see what's over your horizon on my radar.' The group of people so addressed, having heard this pearl of wisdom fall from the user's lips, will then look at each other and say, 'What?' Another of its notable features is the fact that it evolves and mutates constantly as words and phrases rapidly come in to and go out of fashion. The reason for this is quite simple. No glossary of terms is ever published – that would defeat the object of the whole thing in the first place – but it is possible, over a period of time, for the rational and sane, by listening carefully to the context in which the words and phrases are used, to work out roughly what they are intended to mean. ('When I look down your pipeline I can't see what's over your horizon on my radar.' actually means 'I don't know where my next meal is coming from.') When that happens, all is lost, because the clique is no longer exclusive; the excluded have been able to join it. Before that happens, to maintain its purity, the language has to change again, and a new set of words and phrases, usually more ludicrous and obscure than the last set, have to be introduced. The whole thing is obviously absurd, but once it has taken root in an organisation it is very difficult to eradicate, and there can be dangers in denying its addicts access to it. One chief executive did once, accidentally, call a spade a spade; but his doing so drove his company into liquidation quite soon afterwards, as all his executives then spent all of their time and their entire budget for the next financial year on focus groups and projects whose brief was simply to find out what it was he had meant.

Upon entering the actuarial department, the first person John saw was his boss, Roland Smythe. His heart sank at the sight of him. Roland was a substantial man with the build of a rugby player, whose penchant for wearing suits with absurdly wide pin-stripes, and whose broad south London accent made him appear more like a spiv than the head of a serious and sensible department in an equally serious and sensible company. John strongly suspected that the name 'Smythe' was an affectation on Roland's part, designed to prevent his accent from making him pronounce his real surname, Smith, as 'Smiff' – and most of the time it did, except on rare occasions when he forgot to modify his speech, and introduced himself as 'Roland Smyve'.

Like many modern managers and executives, Roland's head was closely shaved, in a style that would have been associated in the past with extreme nationalists and football hooligans – men of violence, all of them. This was now a 'badge of office' sported by male members of the 'in-crowds' and those who aspired to join them. As a fashion it had begun with an ageing chief executive who, fearing that his receding hairline and ever-expanding bald pate would be seen as a sign of the approach of all of the evils he associated with advancing age, and would lessen his power over his underlings, decided to shave his head completely, having connected the vision of voluntary baldness with the ruthlessness and violence of those who had displayed it in the past. It worked and the deterioration of his powers was arrested, so much so that his acolytes opted to imitate him.

Roland was a user of management-speak, but only when it suited him. To be fair to him, he did not use it when talking to members of his department; for that he normally slipped into a dialect strongly associated with the part of south London from which he originated, and containing more than its fair share of words beginning with the letter 'F'. The one phrase, however, to which he had frequent recourse was 'the buzz'. Exactly what he meant by this was unclear, but John and his colleagues had decided that if it was real it could be attributed only to the level of electromagnetic radiation emanating from the large amount of computer equipment located in the building interacting with the metal plate in his head.

Roland had the unhappy knack of seeming always to be around to see John when he arrived late for work, not that it mattered much if he did, because all PLGC employees were allowed the luxury of working flexible hours, so that any time lost in the morning could easily be made up at lunch-time, or in the evening, or on another day altogether. Roland, however, had never let that stop him from making some barbed or (in his opinion) witty comment whenever one of his 'team' arrived after the nine o'clock 'deadline' that he regarded as the last acceptable time for their getting there. This unwelcome and unreasonable attention, for some reason that John could not understand, always made him feel guilty, and that in turn made him annoyed with himself for suffering from it.

'Ah, good morning, John,' Roland said, looking pointedly at his watch. 'So glad you could spare us the time to visit in the middle of your obviously busy morning. That must make you Biddle in the middle! Oh yes, I like that. Biddle in the middle.'

He walked off, laughing and reciting a list of words he could think of that rhymed with Biddle. John, reminded uncomfortably of some of the names by which he had been known in his schooldays, muttered his unnecessary apology at his boss's broad, pin-striped back.

When Roland had gone, John settled down to his day's work, in the orderly and calm world of figures where, as long as the computer system was behaving itself and as long as he got the inputs correct, things happened in a rational and controlled way, outcomes were predictable and there was a sense of satisfaction to be had.

In the middle of the morning a head appeared over the top of the partition beside his desk and a voice invaded his concentration on a string of figures. It was Brian, one of his colleagues.

'Hi, John,' he said, a wry smile on his face. 'Are you joining us for our latest blast of corporate double-speak?'

John looked up, not connecting at first with what Brian had said. 'Oh, bugger!' he said. 'I'd forgotten all about that. Hoping it might go away, I suppose.'

'No such luck,' Brian responded with a grimace. 'You've just got to grin and bear it, like the rest of us. We're going down now.'

The 'us' was the rest of the group of actuarial technicians who worked for Roland, alongside John. They comprised himself, Sue and Patricia – two middle-aged ladies who, like

John, had worked for PLGC and its predecessors for many years – and Brian, the youngster and newcomer in the group, in his mid-twenties and having been with the firm for only three years. The 'down' he referred to was a conference room on the floor below, where the four of them were expected to attend a new training session the Human Resources Department were currently delivering to all lower-level employees. Reluctantly, because they knew what these sessions were like from past experience, they made their way down the stairs, collecting cups of tea or coffee (it was hard to tell which) from the machine in the stair lobby as they went.

As soon as they entered the room they were swooped on and greeted like long lost friends by two young people they had never seen in their lives before. These were Toby and Lynnette, the bouncy, effervescent and intensely annoying 'facilitators' from the Human Resources Department, formerly known as 'Personnel', and which John had mentally renamed 'Inhuman Lack of Resources'. Why the name change? So that people were brought into line with the other 'resources' exploited by companies and became easier to save, presumably.

The four of them sat down on the chairs provided. Toby and Lynnette introduced themselves and the aim of the meeting.

'Hi, everyone!' said Toby. 'I'm Toby and this,' pointing unnecessarily at Lynnette, 'is Lynnette. We're here with you today as your facilitators for the Journey Session of PLGC's Vision for Life Programme, the programme designed to light the way forward for us all into the third millennium. It's serious stuff, I know, but the most important thing for everyone is that it should be fun, even though it's serious. Is that OK with everyone?'

Silence.

'Good. Then I'll hand over to Lynnette to introduce The Journey. Lynnette.'

'Thanks, Toby. That was really great. Hi, everyone!'

More silence.

'Well, first I'd like to tell you how excited I am to be here with you today, helping to lead off this Journey Session, and having so much fun already, doing it. As Toby said, we're all here to have fun – but fun with a serious message.'

Wake me up when the fun starts, thought John, trying hard to stifle the first yawn.

'Now to the serious stuff,' Lynnette continued. 'Toby.'

'Thanks Lynnette. The Journey Session is primarily a continuation of last year's Foundation and Proposition Sessions, which I'm sure you all remember very well. This session will take us all on further, will help to equip us for challenge and change, and then take us on The Journey. I'm very excited about that, and so will you be when we set out on it, but first we'll go into the Regression Session. Lynnette.'

'Thanks, Toby. Wow! Let's all join in now with the Regression Session. This is designed to reiterate and restate the content and findings we got to last year in the Foundation and Proposition Sessions. Not that we should really need to do that, as we all, together, made a commitment to walk the walk, not just talk the talk, didn't we?'

Who's we? thought John. Last year we had two different playschool leaders 'facilitating' us, while you two were still sitting your GCSEs.

'Now we'll begin with your foundation,' said Toby. 'Who can remember what we decided your foundation was?'

You can't for starters: you weren't here, John thought in the silence that followed.

'Come on now,' said Lynnette as though she were speaking to a bunch of reluctant infant school pupils. 'If none of you comes out of your shells and speaks up, then I'm going to have to pick on one of you.'

John had a sudden vision of her, with her fashionable silver-blonde hair tied up in two bunches, one on each side of her apparently empty head, dressed in a pair of blue dungarees with a large red letter 'L' sewn on the front – not a particularly pleasant sight.

'John,' she said, looking straight at him and reading his name from the badge she had insisted each of them wore, 'can you tell me?'

'I do believe, if I'm not very much mistaken, Lynette, that it was a raft of technical excellence,' John answered, trying hard to sound neither bored nor sarcastic.

'Well done, John! That was great!' exploded Toby, without a shred of sarcasm in his voice. 'Now we're cooking with gas!'

I've got to get out of this place, if it's the last thing I ever do! screamed the singer of the song that had suddenly invaded John's head.

'Now we have our foundation, what did we decide we should build on it?' Lynnette asked, with, if that were possible, even more enthusiasm and unbridled excitement than before.

Inside John's cranium, Freddie Mercury began to sing: 'I've got to break free; I've got to break free . . .'

By picking on each of the group in turn, the two facilitators managed, eventually, to establish the fact that the 'firm foundation' supported their four cornerstones of Truth, Trust, Teamwork and Technology, which in turn held up the segments of their 'overarching proposition'. This consisted of two parts. The first was their departmental mission statement, which Roland had decided on their behalf should be 'To boldly go from strength to strength in numbers', presumably because they were in the actuarial department, but with Roland it really was anyone's guess.

'I'd always suspected he was a closet "Trekkie" or something,' Brian had said when it was first launched upon them. 'Now we know for sure.'

The second was the company mission statement, handed down to them by their CEO, the self-styled 'Mentor Mike' (or 'mental Mike' as he was affectionately known by most of his lower-level staff) in the first of a series of chatty communications he had got into the habit of sending out by e-mail to everyone in the company on a regular basis, under the brand name 'Mike's Message'. That mission statement was: 'To make our customers' lives worth having been lived', a worthy ambition by anyone's standards, although its achievement would hardly be likely to impress its supposed beneficiaries, being by then dead. And in between their Raft of Technical Excellence and their Overarching Proposition, supported by their cornerstones the four Ts ('No thanks, mine's a coffee . . . giggle, giggle') was the beating heart of their strength and commitment – their core values and competencies – whatever they were.

With their Regression Session complete and their commitment to the Foundation and Proposition Sessions reiterated, restated and renewed (How appropriate, thought John, because it's all been a load of Rs so far), Toby and Lynnette announced together, in imperfect harmony, that it was time for them to go on The Journey Session.

Hurrah, silently groaned everyone else in the room.

'Where will the journey take us?' asked Toby excitedly.

'What's the journey's purpose?' asked Lynnette animatedly.

Are we nearly there yet? asked John inwardly. And is there a service area we can stop at to get some chips to eat and buy a paper to read?

The group were then asked to 'enter a mind shower session' to answer those two highly important questions, with, of course, Toby and Lynnette working as their facilitators, but on the clear understanding that they, the group, 'owned' the session. In the good old days, when management-speak was in its infancy, the activity they were being asked to join in had been christened 'brainstorming', but now that everyone was thoroughly familiar with that term and it had entered the everyday English language, it had undergone a process of change management and was now known, rather poetically, as a 'mind shower'. (Those who instigated the change hid behind the concept of political correctness, claiming that the term 'brainstorm' was offensive to those who suffered from a medical condition with the same name, whereas those people who still had some kind of grip on reality knew that there was no such condition and that the term had been changed by members of the cliques and 'in-crowds' for the same reason all such terms and words are eventually replaced: to exclude those who do not belong.)

Back in the surreal world of The Journey Session, Brian suggested, somewhat flippantly, that as their departmental mission statement was based on a split infinitive, the journey could well be intended to take them through infinitive and beyond. Toby and Lynnette, having no detectable sense of humour and no grasp of grammar, completely missed both points and just stared mutely at him. Sue, picking up on the theme, as well as having an idea of where this was leading and how long it might take, suggested 'from here to infirmity'. Again there was nothing in the way of a response. John and his colleagues could see that this was going to be a long and gruelling session. They knew from bitter experience that this was far from being 'their' session at all; it was another of Mentor Mike's, and that the answers they were expected to come up with and take 'ownership' of were the ones he had already decided upon.

Knowing that, there were only three ways this could end. The first was for them to get lucky and guess what Mike wanted them to say. The second was to work it out for themselves. The third, and this was usually the quickest way because the workings of the great leader's mind were often obscure to say the least, was to force the two jumping beans at the front to tell them what they should say.

Working together as a group, using a tactic they had developed from their knowledge of Bullshit Bingo, they began to make suggestions, knowing that their facilitators would find it impossible to resist the urge to show off their supposed superiority to those whom they were facilitating.

When the concise history of the Earth comes to be written by dispassionate observers, it will record Bullshit Bingo as having been 'The inevitable consequence of the proliferation of the abhorrence known as "management-speak", in the workplace in the late twentieth and early twenty-first centuries, before sense prevailed and its use was made punishable by death.' For those who do not know, it is a game played by underlings at meetings, as a way of preventing their brains becoming completely fossilised by over-exposure to management-speak. Before the meeting begins, each player is issued with a bingo card which, instead of having a number in each of its squares, has a word from the current vocabulary of management-speak. The cards are kept out of sight below the edge of the table and, as the meeting progresses, the words are crossed out as they are used by various speakers. As in normal bingo, the winners are the first ones to complete a line, or all four corners, or the whole of their card, according to the rules agreed at the outset. Claims for prizes must be made as per regular bingo, but the call of 'House' must be replaced by something more appropriate to the setting of the particular meeting. A cough, a loud escape of wind or a shout of 'hear hear!' might all be thought appropriate, according to the circumstances. In more sophisticated games the holders of the cards can also join in with the speakers, facing the additional challenge of using the words they know they have on their own cards. Adroit players have been known to produce sentences consisting entirely of the words on their cards, simultaneously winning the game and improving their own prospects of promotion.

The game that John and his colleagues played that day was a somewhat different one, being designed to goad those who were not players into giving away the words the others were supposed to guess, something they would do unwittingly as they sought to maintain their superior position. It is invariably successful, as the advocates of management-speak cannot resist using the vocabulary, and if the underlings begin to use it too, the advocates will always respond, in order always to have the last word. If this is kept up for long enough they will run out of words that have not been used and utter the word or phrase they were not supposed to say. Then the game will be over and everyone can return happily to the real world: those who were there in the first place, that is.

True to form, the facilitators had soon given away the words they were not meant to utter. When they did, it was an anti-climax, for all Mental Mike wanted was for PLGC to 'be voted number one for our service at all levels by all of our customers'. That, thought John, might be a little difficult to achieve once a policy becomes payable, since the customer in question will be dead – unless the marketing department plans to employ mediums to conduct their customer satisfaction surveys in the future.

With that, The Journey appeared to be over and the workers were released from captivity to return to their desks. But if they thought that was the end of it they were mistaken, because no sooner had John returned from lunch than along came Lynnette, asking if he was ready for her to conduct the One-to-One Reflection Session he was scheduled for, but had apparently either forgotten about, or deliberately blanked from his memory. She sat down on the spare chair alongside his desk, flattened her skirt, smiled sweetly and asked him how he thought it had all gone in the morning session.

'I thought I detected a little hostility in the room at first,' she told him.

'Did you really?' he said. 'How disheartening that must

have been for you. I must say though, I thought you did a fantastic job of overcoming it and making it such an enjoyable session.'

'Did you think it was?' she said happily. 'I'm so glad, because I thought it went off very well and we all had a lot of fun while achieving so much.'

Sometimes, I believe I must come from a different planet. Either that, or they do, John thought. Lynnette now started to talk about John's three-point plan, what contribution he felt he could make to the success of The Journey and Mentor Mike's vision.

'That,' she said, 'is the personal challenge to you from this morning's work.'

'But Mike's vision' – he almost said it between gritted teeth – 'is for us to be voted number one by our customers. I don't come into contact with any of the customers, so how does it affect me?'

'You're not seeing the bigger picture, John. Not thinking outside the box.'

John was tempted to point out that all big pictures are made up of a myriad tiny details and that, as far as the company was concerned, he was merely one of the details. He was also not sure which box she was thinking of here and, for a second, was tempted to ask her. But his experience of dealing with people like her and her friend Toby had convinced him that they had huge blind spots in their understanding of what he called 'normal' people, one of which was an inability to understand the concept of not understanding the concept. So instead of revealing that he did not understand most of what she was talking about, he just raised his eyebrows and looked at her enquiringly in the hope that it would make him seem intelligent and interested, and encourage her to continue talking. It did – the talking part, at least.

'We all have customers, even if they're not the classic

"external" customers,' Here she raised her hands and wiggled the first two fingers of each one to indicate the quotation marks around the word 'external' as she said it, a mannerism John found intensely annoying. Still he said nothing, so she was forced to continue. 'Think about your workflow pipeline; where it comes from, and where it leads to; where it takes your output when you've finished processing it. If you do that, you'll have identified who your customers are. As you don't deal directly with the external customer base it will almost certainly be someone inside the company, someone internal.'

'The answer to that's simple. It's my boss, Roland, in both cases. He distributes the work to the four of us, and we send it back to him when we've finished. Beyond that it could go to any number of places, but we're never told where or why.'

'In that case,' she said, 'Roland is most definitely your customer.'

What a terrible idea, John thought. For a moment he considered arguing against it by claiming that those beyond Roland, the people the work was ultimately destined to reach, must be a more valid customer-base than the shaven-headed, foul-mouthed, sarcastic moron he was forced to work for. But he didn't. He knew that the best way to get rid of people like Lynnette was simply to agree with what they said and promise to do what they wanted, as long as it did not change anything you actually did. When they had gone, you could carry on in exactly the way you always had, particularly if that way had not changed for years and worked very well.

In that spirit, he agreed that Roland was his 'customer' and that his personal contribution to The Journey would be to make a commitment to ensure that Roland would vote him number one for his customer service for the coming year. Almost as soon as he did, he realised that if a similar conversation were to be held with each of his three colleagues during the course of the afternoon, all four would end up with the major item on their plan as something that three of them could not possibly achieve. Even Lynnette, John thought, must be able to see the stupidity of it. Apparently not.

'So that's the aim of your three-point plan then,' she said, rising to leave. 'Now I've got to agree the same thing with your three work-mates.'

'But that won't work,' John objected. 'The measures that go on these plans are supposed to be achievable. If all four of us have the same goal, three of us can't succeed.'

'We don't use the C word in PLGC, John,' she told him, backing towards the aisle. 'You've all been empowered, remember. It's up to you to make it happen – and if you want it enough, it will!' Then she was gone.

And if it doesn't happen it'll all be my fault, as usual, he thought bitterly. Empowerment – the formalisation by modern managers of the age-old principle: accept the credit and delegate the blame.

So John struggled to complete his three-point plan.

Left to his own devices he would have had a plan with only two points: (1) I will not come into work any more, and (2) I will continue to draw my pay. That would suit him down to the ground.

At five-thirty he gave up the struggle and adjourned to the pub with the others. The Broker and Bitch was the watering hole frequented by the insurance fraternity in South Suburbia, and regarded by people outside those select circles as probably the most boring place in that part of outer London. That evening they were celebrating the departure at the end of the week of a popular PLGC employee who had decided, after a short spell of soul-searching, that her future lay elsewhere.

It was noisy and crowded. The beer was warm. The talk was of football, soap operas, mortgages, pensions, house prices, work, bosses, husbands, wives, kids, cars: the humdrum detritus with which everyday life is cluttered. The woman for whom the leaving party was being held was the last to arrive, owing to pressure of work in her department, which, ironically, was the reason she had decided to leave in the first place.

John stayed there only as long as was decent before heading to the station for the journey home. What pleasures would await him once he got there, he wondered as he walked the well-trodden path he followed twice a day, every day of his working life. What exotic reasons would there be for delays that evening? What absurd or amusing excuses would come tumbling out of the loudspeakers to explain the absence of trains at the platforms to the crowds of people waiting for them to arrive? The answer, he discovered, to his surprise, was none, as everything was running almost exactly to schedule, with a brisk efficiency that was as impressive as it was unusual.

After only a short wait, John was comfortably seated on a train, one of the new ones, a semi-fast service speeding steadily southwards towards its first stop, the airport, after which it would call at Bridges Junction, Southnewtown, Mor-lands and Asham, before carrying on down the line to the coast. The warm evening, the several pints of beer John had inside him and the rhythmic rocking of the train on the smooth, continuously-welded rails soon had him nodding off. His head tipped forward and his chin came to rest on his chest. When he awoke, he found they were slowing down for their arrival at the airport station.

The loudspeakers crackled and clicked, the voice of the guard issued forth – a magnificent one as voices of guards went, with the presence and diction of a classic actor, clear and precise, with beautifully rolled Rs.

'Ladies and gentlemen, we are now apprrroaching High Weald Interrrnational Airrrport Station, our next station-stop on this serrrvice tonight. On leaving the airrrport station, this serrrvice will call at Brrridges Junction, Southnewtown, Morrrlands, Asham, and all stations to Smalltown-on-Sea. Customers for Howard's Heath and all stations to Bigton should change at Brrridges Junction. Customers trrravelling to the rrrest of the world should leave the trrrain and change at High Weald Interrrnational Airrrport Station. I rrrepeat, customers for the rrrest of the world should change at High Weald Airrrport Station, our next station-stop on this serrrvice. Thank you.'

The train stopped; the doors slid open; passengers got off; passengers got on; the doors closed and they were on their way, all without incident. John nodded off again. Bridges Junction and Southnewtown slid by without his noticing and when he woke again they were approaching Morlands. In the carriage ahead of him, several people struggled to their feet, as though getting off was almost too much effort for them at the end of another long day. They made their way towards the exits and waited for the train to stop – only it didn't. It kept on going, straight through the station and out into the open country on the other side.

The guard's voice crackled over the speakers again as the train rushed onwards, leaving Morlands station firmly behind it and the people who had wanted to get off there standing at the still-closed doors looking angry and confused. 'Attention, please! This is an announcement for everyone who thought they were getting off the train at Morlands. I am very sorry. We should have stopped at Morlands station, but the driver's an idiot and he forgot. If you are desiring to go to Morlands tonight I would suggest your best course of action will now be to stay on this train until we reach Asham, then change there for one going back in the opposite direction.'

It was, John supposed, an easy-enough mistake to make and an easy-enough one to understand. The problem must lie, he realised, in the way the semi-fast trains were timetabled on this stretch of the line at this time of the day: for example, a train which stopped at Morlands would run fast through Smallholt; the next one would run fast through Morlands but stop at Smallholt. The driver of this train had just become confused about which one of the two he was driving, and therefore which of the stations he was supposed to stop at – a simple-enough mistake to make. Those who had wanted to get off at Morlands did not share his view, however, and along the length of the train many mobile phones had been pulled out and many angry calls were being made. And they clearly did not share his amusement at the brutal honesty of the guard's announcement in a world of slick, bland, pre-packaged sound bites. This was the real thing – a rarity to savour, be amused by and grateful for.

Their anger was still very much in evidence when they reached Asham, several minutes early, and John got off. The passengers for Morlands got off too, and gathered around the platform staff in a noisy group, wanting to know when they would be able to begin the return journey they had never planned to make in the first place. The echoes of raised voices faded slowly as John ascended the steps onto the bridge, walked over the tracks, and down the other side; on firm ground again; almost home again; looking forward to his ready-meal and spending the rest of the evening in front of the television – after he had recorded the events of the evening in his diary, of course.

3

Week One: Day Three – On a Thursday

It was dawn. At Bridges Junction the thin, pale sunlight spilled in through the windows of the control room, where the scene was as it had been at the same time the day before, the same cast in attendance. The book was lifted from its table again, closed, presented, then re-opened, this time by a different person. Then it was laid back down, covered over and lit up again by the spotlight mounted in the ceiling. The day's work had begun.

Remarkably, nothing went wrong that morning; not for John at any rate. The sun was shining brightly as he made his way to the station, as he boarded the train that arrived at the platform slightly early and left at precisely the time it was scheduled to depart. There was no need for apologies, no need for witty announcements about animals on the tracks and no need for anything more than a minimal number of mobile phone calls to be made, announcing 'It's me; I'm on a train.' As a result of this pleasing punctuality John arrived at his desk on time and so avoided Roland's unwelcome attentions. He slid into his chair with a feeling that it was going to be a better day. His computer started without hanging or crashing and he was soon staring intently at row upon row and column upon column of figures that would have been meaningless to anyone but him and those of his kind.

Slowly he began to manipulate those figures, making this line add up across the row to that figure, then subtracting the sum of the numbers in the column that stood across its right-hand end, as though it were there to stop the row from snaking its way any further towards the edge of the screen, where it might hope to slide unseen into the cover of the plastic surround, and escape.

John did his work in an almost automatic way, pressing keys, moving the computer mouse and clicking away to make numbers augment, diminish or disappear altogether. As he worked, the apparently insoluble problem of the three-point plan came back from the darkest recess of his mind to haunt him. His hope that something would occur to him overnight or in the early part of the morning had deserted him and he found himself no further forward than he had been the evening before.

In the middle of the morning, Roland approached John's PCC-Zee and leant over the top of the partition.

'John,' he said, 'I want you to go to a meeting this afternoon with Perma-way, at their office over the station. Some bullshit to do with health and safety, handed down from the BIC. I'm supposed to be going but I can't be bothered; sounds like a load of crap to me. So I've said you'll go instead. I've sent you the e-mail about it. Go there, tell them to piss off, then get back here as quick as you can, OK?'

John turned back to his computer screen without replying as Roland walked away. He knew that 'no' was not a word his esteemed leader was capable of understanding, unless Roland himself was the one saying it. In any case, a break from the tedium of the office routine would be welcome, even if he had no idea what he might be able to offer to a meeting about a subject like health and safety. He opened the e-mail. It originated from someone at the British Insurance Confederation, the trade association for insurance companies in the UK, in response to a request for assistance from one of the directors at Perma-way, and had found its way to Roland via several directors and departmental heads at PLGC. Perma-way were, it seemed, concerned about the public's perception of their record on health and safety and were launching a project aimed at allowing them to compare their performance with that of others, both inside and outside the rail industry, and with 'the way life worked out in general for the population at large'. As part of that project, they required the assistance of someone with knowledge of, and access to, mortality and accident statistics, and it had occurred to them that such a person might well be found in the actuarial department of one of the larger life insurance companies. To the person at the BIC who had dealt with their enquiry, PLGC had seemed an obvious company to approach, partly because they had always responded helpfully to similar enquiries in the past, but also because their connections in both Europe and the Americas would allow them access to the type of figures Perma-way were looking for, across a substantial part of the developed world. The request that PLGC should send a representative had been accepted by John's bosses, so the first 'Project Definition' meeting had been scheduled for three o'clock that afternoon in the boardroom of the office building above South Suburbia station. Not only did it sound interesting, John thought, but it would also provide him with an opportunity to get off home early for once if it did not take too long. Roland would never know.

So, at just after ten to three, having shut down his computer, John picked up his bag, put on his jacket and made his way out into the warm afternoon sunshine. Walking towards the station at that time of the day was an odd experience for him; the streets which he was more used to seeing during the crowded hustle and bustle of the two daily rush hours were almost deserted. He experienced a strange mixture of guilt, excitement and mild trepidation; what he was about to do was most definitely a step into the unknown.

Overway House was the most recent addition to the skyline of Suburbia, and its black, glass-clad walls loomed over him menacingly as he walked up the slope of the bridge that gave access to both it and the station. The entrance to the offices was located on the left-hand side of the station foyer, behind a transparent glass wall with a revolving door in its centre, through which the reception desk could be seen, with a bank of lifts behind it. John had passed this way on countless occasions on his way to and from his office, but had never taken any notice of either the glass wall or what lay behind it. As he stood in front of it now, preparing to enter, he had the peculiar sensation that it was not there at all normally, and had only materialised, just for him, simply because he now needed it to be there. That feeling stayed with him as he stepped forward to enter through the grand revolving door, only to find that he could not. It appeared to be locked, or broken; either way, it refused to move. He looked up at the receptionist sitting behind the large desk in the foyer behind the glass: a pretty girl, with faultless make-up, wearing expensive and fashionable glasses, her long dark hair pulled back tightly and tied up in a ponytail high on the back of her head. There was a severe and unapproachable look about her, reinforced by the dark, tailored jacket she wore. She was looking down and hadn't seen him. He tapped on the glass. She looked up and made a gesture with one hand indicating either that he should go away, or go somewhere to his right. Stepping back out of the drum of the revolving door, he moved to his right, but failed to find anything that resembled a door. He looked at the receptionist again, to be greeted with an expression that clearly told him she had him classified as some kind of an idiot. She held her hands out in front of her and made a gesture indicating that he should push. John reached out and touched the glass panel in front of him. She smiled sarcastically and nodded slowly in a superior way. He pushed, and the transparent panel, which carried no markings to show that it was a door, swung open to allow him in.

'Hello,' he said, approaching the desk. 'My name's John Biddle. I've come to attend a meeting at three o'clock – on health and safety.'

She looked at a typed list on the shelf of the reception desk in front of her.

'John Biddle,' she repeated slowly, her voice harsh, her accent Scottish. 'Ah, yes. Here we are. Executive Floor. Take the lift on your left, behind me. You'll be met at the top.' Then she picked up a pen and struck through his name with one bold, swift stroke that was almost vindictive in its execution.

John mumbled his thanks and walked towards the lift, wondering whether or not he should say what he was thinking: that it might be helpful if the two doors, broken and working, were marked with signs to that effect. He refrained, however.

As soon as the lift began to move, soft music issued from loudspeakers concealed in its opulent fabric panelling, and John recognised the theme tune Perma-way used as the background to all its television advertisements. Then a familiar voice, that of one of Britain's most glamorous and, in his opinion, sexy, actresses began speaking, as though directly to him.

'Welcome on board the executive lift for this short trip up to the Permanent Way Agency's Executive Floor. Relax and enjoy the ride, brought to you today by The Permanent Way Agency; keeping trains on track for the benefit of Britain.'

The lift came to a stop on the top floor before he had realised it had started to move, so smooth was it – unlike some of the trains that ran over the Agency's tracks each day – and the doors slid open. John stepped out and found himself in an enclosed area, deep-pile carpet underfoot, expensive wooden panelling on the walls, and three sets of double doors leading off. All the doors were closed. Behind him the lift doors also closed and the faint whirring sound of machinery in motion told him it was descending, taking its seductive soundtrack back to the ground floor to greet someone else, perhaps. Not knowing quite what he should do, John waited to see what, if anything, would happen next. It was always a good tactic, he found, and one that had served him well over the years. It led to something of a quiet existence for those who adopted it as a way of getting through life, but it gave them some degree of protection against nasty surprises. They would never be the ones who fell down holes in the dark, for example, or were attacked by a mad axe-murderer lurking behind the half-open door. Unfortunately, it also meant they were not the ones who collected the rewards reserved for those who come first at things, and often left them sorting through the débris of whatever it was that no-one else had claimed or appeared to want. It also left them standing on their own in deserted lift lobbies from time to time, waiting to see what would happen next.

Several minutes passed. John began to get impatient; the bold and assertive part of his personality began to fight against the meek and retiring part. The sensible thing would be to go to each of the doors in turn and see which one opens onto the meeting you're here to attend, the brave part told him, knowing that the meek part would counter with a strong argument about the need to avoid embarrassment at all costs.

Go on, you wimp. Open a door. You can't stand here forever.

But what if it's the wrong one? I wouldn't like that, and I'd get myself all flustered.

They argued the pros and cons for several minutes more,

then reached an agreement. John coughed loudly. One of the doors on his left was opened and a tall, thin, grey-haired man in a dark suit emerged.

'Mister Biddle?' he said, holding his hand out to be shaken. 'My name is Stephen Dent. I'm the project leader with The Permanent Way Agency, chairing the meeting this afternoon. They phoned up from reception to say you'd arrived. I'm sorry we kept you waiting. There were some preliminary details to be sorted out before we got started, but we're ready now, so come on in and meet everyone.'

So saying he shepherded John through the open door into the room beyond, where there were nine other men, already seated around a large, oval, and very expensive-looking meeting table. John was shown to an empty chair at the end nearest the door and supplied with a cup of tea and a plate of biscuits to choose from. The meeting began.

It started with a round of introductions. Apart from one of them, and John himself, everyone present was some kind of director at Perma-way. Either they were all very high-powered people, John thought, or the title 'director' was an overused one in their organisation. The preponderance of sharp, designer suits and monogrammed shirt pockets on view suggested the former. Perma-way were obviously taking this project pretty seriously. That view was reinforced when Stephen Dent began to speak.

'Gentlemen,' he said, 'may I introduce you to John Biddle, a Phace, Liss and Gray man, who's here to help us with our actuarial input to the project.' He turned to John, who was trying to work out whether or not he had just been insulted. 'Everyone here is a member of The Permanent Way Agency's Southern Regional Management Board, with the exception of the gentleman sitting directly opposite you.' He indicated a nondescript person dressed in an old-fashioned blazer and what looked like some kind of regimental tie. 'He,' Stephen Dent continued, 'is Mr. Adrian Wright, and he works for a company called Amalgamated Risk Services (Europe) Limited, who are one of our external partners on the project, providing expertise that we don't have in-house.'

Mr. Wright inclined his head slightly in John's direction. John returned the compliment with the smallest of smiles. Only later did it occur to him that Dent had carefully omitted mentioning what kind of services Mr. Wright might be providing to Perma-way.

'Now I'll ask everyone else to introduce themselves briefly, so you know who they are and have some idea of their involvement in the project.' He began with himself. 'I'm Stephen Dent, as you know. I'm the Financial Director for the division. My role is a very straightforward one: to make sure we operate at a profit.'

He nodded to the next man at the table, who took his turn.

'My name is Bill Taylor. I'm the Commercial Director. I'm responsible for the development and implementation of our marketing and sales strategy.'

'Colin McFee,' the next announced brusquely. 'Operations Director. I make sure the trains run on time.' He gave a laugh – or was it more like a snort?

No you don't, thought John, and grimaced.

'David Law, Communications Director,' said the next one. 'I make sure we maintain the positive image of the company in the eyes of the world at large.'

I'm not sure you've got one of those to maintain, John thought.

'I'm Irwin Lee, SHEQ Director, responsible for safety, health, environmental protection and quality assurance systems on the railway.'

Can't argue with that, John thought.

'Peter Davis, Infrastructure Services Director. My remit is to keep the track, signals, power supplies and the like up and running, day in and day out.'

Big job – and the very best of luck to you with it.

'I'm Alan Perkes. I'm the Director of Human Resources. I'm the "people person".' And as he said 'people person' he did that oh-so-annoying thing with his fingers.

Ugh!

'Hello. I'm Gordon Harper. I'm the IT Director for the division – keeping all the computers working.

And last but not least. . .

'Richard Keane, External Liaison Director. I manage contacts with other stakeholders in the railway – The Department of Transport, OFFTOSS, the train operators, other franchise-holders and the like – keeping those relationships running along smoothly.'

And if it works with them, could you try doing the same thing with the trains please?

While the others were talking, John had, at first, felt the urge to make notes, knowing that he would never be able to remember who everyone was and what they did. He realised gratefully, however, that everything he needed to know in that respect had been set out at the top of a sheet of paper lying on the table in front of him, just above the proposed agenda for the meeting. Then it was his turn to speak.

'As Mr. Dent said earlier, I'm John Biddle. I work as an actuarial technician for PLGC. I was asked to come to the meeting today in response to the request for help you made via the BIC. I'm not sure anyone at PLGC realised the importance you obviously attach to the project you're launching here. If they had, I'm sure they would have sent a more senior person, and I apologise if I find I can't help you fully. However, I do have access to the sort of information you described in your original request, so I hope I shall be of some use to you.'

It all came out in something of a hurry, as things usually did when John was nervous. Stephen Dent spoke again.

'Thank you gentlemen, and thanks for being so candid

John. It's much appreciated. You're not to worry yourself about title or position here. Most of us came up through the ranks, as it were, so you've no call to worry about fancy titles and the like. If, as you say, you have access to the information we're looking for, then you're exactly the right man to help us out. Shall we get going then? Bill, perhaps you'd like to start us off with an explanation of how all this came about.'

'Thanks, Stephen,' said Bill. 'For a number of years now, the public at large have been growing progressively more interested in safety and safety performance – in all areas of life, not just in transport. As their interest has grown, it's been realised that safety itself can be used as a sales tool. The airlines pioneered it, with those among them having the best safety records finding that, when all else is equal, publicising their good record can lead to increased utilisation ratios, more efficient working and, therefore, higher profits.'

Bill stopped and looked to his colleague, David Law, Communications Director, to continue. He obliged.

'Now we feel the time is right for us to do the same thing. In the past, rail advertising campaigns have tended to concentrate on various aspects of the travel experience that were hard to quantify but were easy to knock and mock. Take the last three major campaigns of the British Rail era.' As he spoke he reached out and pressed several buttons on a small console in front of him. The lights in the room faded and an image appeared on an area of the far wall. Several of them had to turn round to be able to see the three TV adverts that had been made for the campaigns David Law had referred to. When all three had run their course and the images had faded, David spoke again.

'The message from the first advert was 'We're getting there', only they weren't, and it was all too easy to show that they weren't. In the second, we were encouraged to

'Let the train take the strain'. Well, it was the common perception at the time that, for many regular rail users, it was the train itself that was causing much of the strain in the first place. And finally, we were told that 'This is the age of the train', which wasn't a particularly wise thing to say, as much of the rolling stock being used at the time was life-expired and should have been replaced long before then. A new advertising campaign is needed, but it's our intention to produce one free from the problems of those you've just seen illustrated. Irwin.'

'Thanks, David. After thinking about it long and hard, the board decided we needed a campaign that would highlight the quality of the experience of travelling by rail, but not give critics anything they could snipe at too readily. We considered a wide range of options, before settling on the one we're launching here today. What we've decided to do is mimic the best features of the airlines' campaigns based on their safety records. We think that those campaigns were very clever, particularly when they started to compare their safety records with other aspects of life, and not just with one another. They began highlighting interesting, witty and little-known facts – for example, the one that tells us that more people have died in the UK in the last ten years while putting their trousers on than have perished in air crashes anywhere in the world involving UK-based aircraft. We think that by benchmarking our safety record against a wide range of lifestyle activities, not just against the safety records of our competitors, and with a careful and considered marketing campaign to emphasise what we see as our key differentiators, we can establish in the eyes of the public and the minds of our stakeholders the fact that we are a best-of-breed organisation with respect to safety. In other words, elevate our safety record to become our key public KPI, but always make sure that it compares favourably with whatever we choose to contrast it. Having done that, we'll be in a position to exploit the linkage that's been shown to be made in the minds of the man and woman in the street between one quality indicator and others. In other words, if an organisation is good enough to get its safety management right, it must automatically be getting the other things that matter right as well. That, in a nutshell, is the challenge we've set for ourselves.'

While Irwin was speaking, John's management-speak alarms had been sounding loudly. With mention of benchmarking, key differentiators, stakeholders, best-of-breed, quality indicators and challenges, all in the same short speech, he was pretty sure Irwin was mocking his colleagues: either that or he was playing a winning round of Bullshit Bingo. And using the phrase 'key KPI', even with the word 'public' in the middle of it, must be the Bullshit Bingo equivalent of placing a word containing the Z and the Q on both the triple letter score and triple word score boxes in one and the same turn in Scrabble. The tla (three letter acronym) 'KPI' stood for 'Key Performance Indicator', so the term Irwin had just used or invented, must mean 'key key performance indicator', reminiscent of the classic piece of vintage management-speak, from way back in the 1980s, 'at this present moment in time', meaning 'now'.

Irwin continued. 'Through the various railway operators' forums we belong to we have access to accident and fatality statistics for all our major competitors: French railways, German railways, those in Belgium, Holland, etcetera – and, of course, our own.'

I doubt that the average passenger would see the railways in other countries as your competitors here, John thought. Your true competitors are the other means of transport which cover the same routes as you do, like buses, aircraft and cars.

'What we would like to obtain is a wider access to statistics that would enable us to make comparisons between our levels of safety and those inherent in other activities, like making a car journey, or travelling by bus, or taking a skiing holiday, or simply staying at home. Then we'd be able to say that travelling by train is as safe as, say, sitting at home watching the news on TV, or much safer than going skiing. I don't know at the moment if it is, or isn't. Those are just examples of the types of thing we want to be able to do and say.'

'It might also be helpful to examine the safety records of those other countries by another means, just in case they're being economical with the truth in terms of the figures they submit to the forums,' he added as an afterthought.

As are you, thought John, guessing that Perma-way's awareness of their own acts of deception probably lay at the root of their apparent distrust of the others.

Lee interposed with a question, put to John, that the others around the table were keen to hear answered. 'Do you think, Mr. Biddle, based on what you've heard so far, that you'll be able to help us?'

John was silent for several seconds as he marshalled his thoughts, then smiled at the expectant faces around the table.

'Yes,' he said. 'I think it should be possible to provide you with just what you're looking for. PLGC operates in a large number of countries around the world, basically providing life and health insurance, with life cover forming significantly the larger part of the business. Premiums in both areas of business are determined almost exclusively by actuarial calculations, and in order to allow us to carry out that work, we collect vast amounts of data every year. The data is loaded into powerful computer databases which record as much information as possible about the circumstances of the accident, or illness, or death, that causes any particular claim to be made. The way the data is input, using very sophisticated methods of coding and cross-referencing, enables a vast range of information to be extracted, in a large variety of configurations and formats. That's the information the actuaries then use to classify and categorise risk and calculate appropriate levels of premium.'

'To make sure your fat-cat directors and shareholders get their fat bonuses and dividends each year, no doubt,' chipped in someone who appeared to hold a grudge of some kind against insurance companies. There was always one, and there always had been, at every meeting of this kind John had ever attended. Stephen Dent frowned at the cause of this unwanted interruption.

'I don't know how you might want the information broken down,' John said, 'but it's possible to categorise deaths in a number of ways: accident, illness or suicide, for example. I assume you'll want suicide included?'

'Definitely,' Irwin Lee replied quickly. 'In view of the issues we have with open platform edges, it's an essential.'

'OK,' said John. 'Then below that we can sub-classify by cause: different illnesses, different accident causes, different methods of committing suicide. That's where you start to see the type of information you were talking about earlier coming out.'

By talking it through in detail, the information Perma-way wanted was closely defined, so that John would be able to interrogate PLGC's databases efficiently when he got back to his desk. They then went on to discuss how the data should be presented and transferred to Perma-way's own computer systems so that they could begin to use it. This was something for the IT Director to sort out with John. It was decided that John would return early the following week, bringing the information he had prepared thus far on compact discs.

Agreement having been reached, the meeting was effectively over and it was John's cue to leave. Perma-way's directors knew what they wanted, and they now knew that John could supply them with it, so they were happy. John knew what he had to do, so he was happy too. Impressed by their slick style of presentation and their confident sense of authority and purpose, it was easy for John to be happy; it all seemed so sensible, so plausible. Only later would events reveal it to have been a pretence, a sham designed to conceal their real purpose in getting their hands on the information with which John had promised to supply them.

John was escorted back to the lift by Stephen Dent, who shook his hand warmly, thanked him for his time and looked forward to seeing him again in the early part of the following week. The lift took him smoothly down to the ground floor, caressing, massaging him gently with its music as it did, and wishing him a safe and pleasant onward journey as he left it. The frosty-faced receptionist, however, had not thawed since he had last seen her and brushed away his query about signing out with a dismissive gesture of her hand. Presumably, her wishes and those expressed by the lift were not the same.

John pushed his way through the unmarked glass door into the station entrance, congratulating himself on his early escape from work. Now he just had to hope that the trains were behaving themselves when he got to the station concourse. Having got there, he could see straightaway that all was not well. The foyer, normally a place most people passed through quickly on their way to the platforms, was full almost to bursting point, the crowds standing motionless, staring blankly up at the destination boards. The boards themselves were far from blank. Underneath almost every train listed was the word that every commuter dreads to see: 'Delayed'. This is the word employed by the railway companies when even they have no idea what is happening on the parts of the network for which they are responsible.

John joined the throng and stared up at the boards above the ticket gates, like everyone else there, trying to work out what was going on and what his options were for getting home in the shortest possible time. It was clear from the times of the trains being displayed that the whole of the network around South Suburbia was suffering from considerable disruption, trains running well over an hour late in most cases. After a moment's thought, he made his way down onto platform three, from where the first train heading south, towards the airport and Bridges Junction, was scheduled to leave. Down on the platform the crush was even worse than it had been up in the foyer, people standing eight or nine deep, but in reasonably well-ordered and patient rows. John stood quietly at the back and waited. After a while the public address system burst into life.

'Attention please! This is a customer announcement. South Coast Regional Trains would like to apologise for the delays currently being experienced on your journeys out of South Suburbia tonight. This is due to a major power and signalling failure in the Bridges Junction area, which the engineering staff of our network partner, The Permanent Way Agency, are currently working to rectify. Please be assured that every effort is being made to correct this problem, and we hope to have you on your way again as soon as we possibly can. In the meantime, please listen carefully to station announcements, as all trains are currently subject to delay, platform alteration and cancellation at short notice. Thank you.'

Shortly after the end of that announcement, the first train to arrive since John had got there rolled in and came to a stop alongside the platform. It quickly filled up, but was of no use to John as it did not go anywhere near Bridges Junction. Soon more trains began to arrive from London, heading south, and the crowd started to thin a little. Each arrival was accompanied by an announcement from the loudspeakers, directing that customers for this or that station should join this train and change at some other station, while customers for somewhere else should remain on the platform and await the next train to arrive, which was understood to be only ten minutes away, customers this . . . , customers that . . . , customers something else . . . In front of John, one man turned to another standing beside him.

'I've just worked out why they call us customers and not passengers, you know,' he said.

'Oh, really! Why's that then?'

'Because if they still called us passengers they might feel obliged to take us somewhere!' said the first, and they both laughed.

Many a true word is spoken in jest, thought John ruefully.

The next announcement gave John some hope.

'Attention please! This is an announcement for customers waiting for trains calling at stations from Bridges Junction to Smalltown-on-Sea. Trains on the Bridges Junction to Smalltown line will be starting from Bridges Junction this evening as a temporary measure to ease congestion at South Suburbia. Customers for stations from Southnewtown to Smalltown should take the first available train from this station and change at Bridges Junction. The next train for Bridges Junction is expected to arrive at platform three in approximately four minutes' time.'

When the promised train did arrive, John and half the other people on the platform tried to cram themselves onto it, leading to disappointment for some, and adding to its already heavily-loaded condition. John was amongst the lucky ones. Once all the doors had been closed it was sent on its way by the harassed platform staff, who, understandably, were looking forward to the end of their shifts even more that day than they normally did. John, hot, crushed and uncomfortable, wedged in place between other, similarly discomfited commuters, looked forward to the train arriving at Bridges Junction. As the journey proceeded the crush eased somewhat. At each station a few more people got off. Even that was not an easy process, though, as the passengers had not got on in the order in which they needed to get off, so there was a certain amount of struggling and shuffling about required whenever it stopped.

At the airport station the face of the TV monster leered down, as if knowing what the sardines in their passing tin cans were suffering.

Going nowhere? Go shove-yer-phone, thought John.

At Bridges Junction the doors flew open, disgorging hundreds of people onto the tarmac surface of platform number five.

'Bridges Junction, this is Bridges Junction,' came the cry from the loudspeakers. 'The train now at platform five is for Howard's Heath and all stations to Bigton. Customers for Southnewtown and all stations to Smalltown-on-Sea should make their way via the underpass to platform one where there is a train waiting for you. Hurry along please as this service is ready to leave.'

The announcement was greeted by a murmur of raised voices, groaning and muttering in unison. The reason was simple. While the underpass was wide, with plenty of space for any number of people to pass through it together and the ramp leading up onto platform one from the underpass, though not quite so generously proportioned, was still of a reasonable width, the wooden staircase that ran down from platform five into the underpass was steep, narrow, and had a right-angled bend halfway down, features unlikely to facilitate the swift movement of a crowd in a hurry.

John was lucky. He found himself near the top of the steps when the Bigton train came to a halt, and was one of the first people down them, through the underpass, up the ramp and onto the train waiting at platform one. Knowing that this part of his journey would be a crowded one too, he found, and thankfully folded himself into, an empty seat.

The train John had just boarded was another of the old, slam-door variety. Neither the train crew nor the platform staff had control over most of the doors; the passengers, however, did. What the passengers did was leave the doors open as they got on, knowing that there were many hundreds more people behind them who also wanted – and deserved – to board the train.

The only person who did not seem to realise this was the pimply youth who had been given the task of making sure that this train left the station at the time it was supposed to. As more and more passengers emerged from the head of the ramp and climbed wearily onto the rapidly-filling train, he could be seen walking backwards and forwards in an agitated manner, slamming the doors firmly shut, only to find them being thrown open again by the next person wanting to board. So indoctrinated was this particular lad, and so infected by the fear of fines for late-running was the train-operating company that employed him, that he lost his head completely. Abandoning his attempt to close all the doors by himself, he stalked over to the balustrade running along the side of the ramp, leant over and shouted at the crowds still making their way up from the underpass.

'Get a fucking move on!,' he bawled. 'This fucking train's ready to fucking leave.'

Before he knew what was happening to him, he was pinned to the side of the train, a large hand holding him warmly by the throat, with his feet hardly touching the ground. The shaven-headed, pin-striped suit, not unlike Roland, who held him there thrust his angry face close to that of the pimply youth.

'You can't fucking swear at the fucking passengers', he shouted, so loudly that everyone on the station (and quite a few not on it) could hear him.

The first bout of raised voices had alerted the rest of the station staff to the fact that something was amiss, and they now came to the lad's rescue, before anything more than shouting broke out. Seconds later, the supervisor had managed to placate the angry passengers, assuring them that the train would not leave until everyone who wanted to travel was on board, and himself had the pimply youth held firmly by the throat up against the side of the train.

'You can't fucking swear at the fucking customers!' he shouted, echoing the words used by the irate passenger only seconds before.

That was the last piece of excitement on John's journey. The train stayed where it was until all the passengers had boarded and all the doors were closed. Then it was waved off by the supervisor. Of the pimply youth no more was seen. Asham was reached in due course without further incident, but it must have been, John thought, a bumper day for calls on the mobile phone networks.

4

Week One: Day Four – On a Friday

The last working day of the week dawned bright and clear over Asham, the run of fine weather continuing, with the promise of more to come over the weekend. John's train came in and departed on time for the second day running, in spite of the chaos that had engulfed the network the evening before.

John stepped on board and sat down next to another man from Asham who was opening up his copy of that morning's local newspaper. Like so many of us, John could not resist surreptitiously reading the main article on the front page, after the banner headline had caught his eye:

'LOCAL AUTHOR BANNED FROM TRAINS IN ROW OVER COMIC NOVEL'

The author referred to, a local man who commuted regularly on the trains in the area had, it seemed, published a satirical novel based on diaries he had kept over the years recording details of all of the delays and inconveniences he and his fellow travellers had suffered at the hands of the railways in that time, along with the excuses the train operators had offered. Now the train company, embarrassed by the book's success and the author's popularity, had written to him suggesting that, if he found the service they offered so little to his taste, perhaps it would be best if he took his custom elsewhere and chose not to travel with them in the future, leaving space for others more appreciative of their efforts.

John was amazed. He had been keeping his diaries for years as well, recording exactly the same information as that described in the article, strictly for his own amusement, without ever thinking that anything more might be made of it. For what was possibly the very first time, he saw one of life's opportunities passing him by, without ever having noticed, until then, its existence. He felt a pang of regret that it had been someone else who had been smart enough to benefit. And, judging from the tone of the article, the author was benefiting very nicely indeed from the idea and his development of it. John turned away, trying to push the thought to the back of his mind and concentrate on reading his book for the rest of the journey, but he was not entirely successful and got off the train in Suburbia feeling gloomier and more discontented with his lot than he had been for a long time.

In the office, Roland was as obnoxious as usual, particularly when he found out what Perma-way had asked John to do.

'You've told them you'll do what?' he shouted, so loudly that almost everyone on the floor stopped what they were doing and looked round to see what was going on. 'I told you to tell them to piss off, then get back here and carry on with your work. But instead of that you agree to do something that's got bugger all to do with us and will take who knows how long to finish, especially for a dumb-arse like you.'

'But I couldn't very well say no,' John protested, ignoring the insult. 'You'd agreed that I should go, and the message they got back telling them someone would be there made it clear that it had been agreed to at a high level. Judging by the representatives from Perma-way, they were expecting someone quite senior from our side.'

Roland laughed sarcastically. 'They must have been disappointed when you rolled up. You wouldn't be mistaken for anyone like that in a month of Sundays.'

'So what do you want me to do?' John snapped, his anger rising. 'Do what they want, or send them an e-mail saying that you've told me I'm not allowed to.'

Roland stood and thought about it for a moment or two, eventually realising that if John now failed to do what had been agreed it would reflect badly on him, and that any message he sent now would have to be passed upwards via the various directors who had been involved at PLGC in the first place, which might not be helpful to someone who was hoping for advancement in his career.

' OK,' he said slowly, 'do the sodding work they want you to, but do it as quickly as you can, then get on with what I actually pay you to do.'

John seethed quietly as Roland walked away from him, then settled down to the task the Perma-way directors had set for him, beginning by making up a file for the papers he had been given the afternoon before and for the notes he was about to make on the methods he would employ to find the information he needed. He looked at the printed sheets he had taken home with him from the meeting in Overway House, that set out the agenda, and the names and contact details of the people he had met and was now working with – for the time being, at least. They formed a high-powered group within Perma-way: stephen.dent@southern.tpwa.co.uk; all the others @southern.tpwa.co.uk; except for one, the odd man out in every respect, whose e-mail address made John almost choke with laughter when he saw it: a_wright@arse.com. Adrian Wright, who would from that time forward be thought of by John as 'a right arse', with, as it would turn out, some justification.

When Roland was well and truly out of sight, a head appeared over the top of the partition alongside John's desk.

'Morning, John,' Brian greeted him cheerily. 'I would say 'good' morning, but I know you've been spoken at already by the irascible Roland, and as I know that merely seeing that man is enough to spoil anyone's day, actually having to converse with him is unlikely to make things any better.'

'You can say that again,' John agreed.

'Why do we all put up with it?' Brian asked rhetorically, because he already knew the answer: they all needed the money and they were too dull, or too stuck in their ways to do anything else, or go looking anywhere else for a job.

'Speaking of pain, suffering and futility, how's your three-point plan coming on?' Brian asked.

'Missing a few points at the moment,' John told him gloomily. 'Beyond the need to make myself Roland's number one, I literally can't see the point. How's yours?'

'Pretty much the same. I come here to work, to get paid, and to go home again. If I manage to brighten the journey of any of my fellow travellers as we wend our weary way through the trials and tribulations of the working day together, I'll go to bed each night a happy and joyful man, and know I'm a small step nearer to my hoped-for place in heaven.'

John knew his friend was joking, because he had never come across a less religious individual than Brian.

'Get back to work, Brian,' John told him. 'Before your cynicism rubs off on the rest of us. And if you manage to see the point rather than the light, you *will* share it with the rest of us, won't you?'

'Of course I will. It would be against my humanist principles to leave you all floundering while I basked alone in the light of the wonder of our mentor's vision.' He turned and strode away, laughing.

John went back to his work.

When he had something interesting to do, John found

that the time passed quickly, and this day proved to be one of those that rushed past without his noticing where the minutes and the hours had gone to. By the end of the afternoon it was clear he was going to be able to do a very good job indeed for Stephen Dent and his fellow Perma-way directors.

His outline interrogation of PLGC's databases had quickly shown him that everything he had said at the meeting the day before was true: that he would be able to supply data showing, in some detail, how, why, how often and where people died, whether those deaths were natural or otherwise. He was also able to do the same thing, although on a somewhat less extensive scale, with accidents and illnesses. Then he extended his search into information and databases held by other organisations who put their statistical records into the public domain: government departments and bodies; publicly-funded organisations; companies and corporations that had moral or ethical outlooks and believed in open and honest policies when it came to airing their dirty linen in public. Interestingly, Perma-way was not among them, although OFFTOSS was, so data was available to allow comparisons to be made both with other railway operators and other means of transport.

Then he began to compile the databases he would be handing over to Perma-way when he next met them. This was the part that would take him the most time; contrary to Roland's expectations, it would not be quick. To begin with, all the information had to be reduced to a common baseline so that it could be judged comparatively.

After giving the matter considerable thought, he decided that several baseline measures were needed for the various types of information he was handling: the figures that related to the various modes of travel expressed in terms of numbers of accidents and deaths per passenger kilometre travelled, and the other accident, mortality and illness figures per head of the population. Ideally, he would have liked to have linked those two sets of figures together by using anything he could find on the estimated number of hours that people were exposed to the cause of their accident, death or illness, but in the end that proved to be too difficult to achieve, so he had to abandon the idea – much to his annoyance as it would have been a real feather in his cap to have been able to do it.

All that work, enjoyable though it proved to be, was time-consuming, and put him further and further adrift from Roland's instruction to do what was needed quickly, then get back to his 'proper' work. In the middle of the afternoon the pin-striped dictator hove into view around the end of the partition alongside John's desk to find out how things were going and when they would be finished.

'What are you fiddling about with now, Biddle?' he demanded.

John groaned inwardly, knowing what was coming next.

'Biddle the fiddle,' Roland said, entering another of his creative, poetic moods.

Thick as pudding, but never a disappointment, John thought.

'Finished playing and got back to some real work yet, have you?'

'No, sorry,' said John. 'It's taking quite a long time to sort out.' He knew he should be more forceful, and not apologise for something that was clearly not his fault, but he did not think he had it in him just then to do anything else. His instinctive response to Roland's next insult proved him wrong, however, as he lashed back at his tormentor.

'Do you do it deliberately to spite me, Biddle, or are you really as thick and sluggish as you make yourself out to be? Looking at what you've done here so far,' pointing at John's computer screen, 'a half-wit ten-year-old from the academy for dimwits could have done it quicker.'

'And so could I if you didn't keep interrupting me to find out how it's going and how far I've got with it. If you'd just leave me alone I'd get on twice as fast!'

Stepping back in mock shock, Roland crowed, 'Ooh, get you! Meek and mild John Biddle snaps back at his nasty, oppressive boss.' Then, leaning forward, he added in a quiet and threatening voice, 'If I were you I'd be careful how you speak to me, John. Don't forget that your primary aim for the year, according to your plan, is to make me vote for you as my number one. Well, at the moment I can tell you that you're down somewhere at around number ten, and that's in a group of just four of you, so you've got a lot of grovelling and catching up to do!'

Now John was really angry, but before he could think of anything cutting to say in reply, Roland had turned round and walked off, denying him the opportunity, unless he wanted to stand up and shout at the back of his boss's head.

If only, he mused, I'd had the gumption to turn my railway diaries into a best-selling book. If only I was the one now banned from the trains, from the sheer hell of commuting, from all of this, confined to the comfort of my own home while I watched the book sales go on rising and the money coming in.

Because, he supposed, it was at the forefront of his mind as a result of the work he was doing, John started to think of the nasty, painful things he wished might happen to Roland over the course of the coming weekend: accidents, illnesses or painful death. He was shocked that he could be so vindictive, even if it was all in his head. Then he imagined himself in court, up before the judge to defend himself against the accusation that he had been the cause of Roland Smythe's untimely demise, justifying himself by reciting the catalogue of abuses he had been subjected to at the hands of this overbearing tyrant. For a moment it made him feel better; then it turned in on itself and made him feel worse, because he knew it was all a fantasy and that in the real world, the one he had to deal with every day, nothing had changed.

He carried on working until the end of the afternoon, the gloom sitting heavily upon him, then got up and left his office without saying 'Goodnight' or 'Have a nice weekend' to anyone, glad that it was Friday evening. He walked briskly to the station, feeling the exercise dissipate his tension and stress, expecting the worst from the trains, but pleasantly surprised to find that they were all running smoothly and to time. This mild euphoria continued all the way back to Asham, where he got off the train, strolled over the foot bridge, down the steps and back to his house, glad that the week was over and the weekend had begun. Nothing was cancelled, nothing was delayed or late, but that had done nothing to stem the tide of mobile phone calls as the train arrived, on time, in Asham station.

'Hello, it's me! You'll never guess what: it's Friday and the train's just got in on time. No, honestly – it's true! Yeah, it's gonna be a great weekend. See you in a minute or two.'

5

Weekend One

Typical weekends in John's life were conducted in very much the same vein as his typical weeks – that is, in accordance with schedules and routines, rigidly adhered to. Having such a regimented style of life is generally only possible under one of three distinct sets of circumstances: being single and living alone; living with a partner who is strongly like-minded; being a member of the armed forces. As we have seen, John was firmly in the first of these categories: he had only himself to please, which he did by sticking to schedules and routines which had been tried and tested over the course of many years and made him feel comfortable and safe. There was, he thought, enough uncertainty, turmoil and disruption at large in the world without its having to invade his calm and settled lifestyle; he had no desire for change. He generally woke up at around 6:30 a.m., through both summer and winter, and got up almost straightaway. Lounging around in bed was a waste of time: besides, if he stayed there too long of a morning it made him feel fidgety and out of sorts for the rest of the day.

This Saturday, having got out of bed, showered and dressed, John took himself downstairs to eat his breakfast at his dining-room table with the Saturday paper open in front of him. Saturday was the one day of the week he did take a newspaper, one of the heavyweight broadsheets, delivered to his door by the local newsagent. It was a substantial item, massive enough to land on the doormat in his entrance hall with a reassuring thud, extensive enough to provide him with reading matter through most of the weekend, and authoritative enough to convince him that what he was reading was the truth about the world outside his door.

Not like the tabloid press, he told himself, which is full of sensationalism, political spin and bare breasts – more like comics for grown-ups than newspapers for adults.

If he found himself in want of the particular kind of light relief offered by such publications, he could always snatch surreptitious glances at those being read by the people on either side of him on the train, as most of us do from time to time. So he sat there at his table, eating his breakfast and drinking his tea, scanning the headlines and reading those stories he found of most interest.

When he had finished eating, he collected his breakfast things, took them into the kitchen and put them in the dishwasher. He pulled his shopping bags out of the cupboard by the sink, where he kept them when they were not in use, took them into the hallway and stood them beside the front door. After cleaning his teeth, exchanging his slippers for a pair of shoes and pulling on his summer-weight casual jacket – just in case it was not as warm outside as it looked – he collected the bags, stepped out through his front door, pulled it firmly shut behind him and set out along the road in a resolute manner. John's mood that day was not one of his best, as the determined way in which he marched away from the house might have revealed to anyone who knew him well. Normally, he spent his weekends either in a good mood or, at worst, in what he tended to think of as a neutral mood – neither too happy on the one hand, nor too grumpy on the other. This weekend was, he knew, going to be different; a dark shadow having been cast over it by Roland Smythe. The bitter aftertaste of his exchange with Roland still hung over John, clouding his mood, a mood that he feared could only get worse as the weekend wore on and Monday morning loomed ever closer. For this reason he was feeling particularly intolerant of everything and everybody as he walked into the town centre that morning and approached the portals of his local supermarket.

His arrival was, as usual, timed to coincide with the opening of the doors, giving him the chance to get round, get out and get home before the dense crowds of Saturday shoppers arrived. That day the doors were late in opening, as they sometimes were (just to spite him) and he was forced to join the back of a queue that had formed in front of them, composed mainly, it seemed, of old-age pensioners – the so-called 'grey panthers'.

Why panthers? he asked himself, thinking the comparison between this queue of doddery old specimens of humanity and the lithe, athletic felines of the jungle could not be more inappropriate. And why do old people seem to like queuing up so much? he wondered, staring idly at the back of the twenty or so grizzled, grey, blue-rinsed or bald heads that stood between him and the entrance to the store. Why do the great legions of the retired feel the need to arrive everywhere they go so early? So early that they have then to queue up and wait. As they're retired and don't have to spend their days going to work like the rest of us, they could do more or less anything they wanted to, any time they wanted to. Is it because they have less time left than the rest of us and, because of that, they want to get everything done as soon as possible, before that time runs out for them? Or could it simply be that, after a lifetime of having to rub shoulders with the rest of us, they are fed up to the back teeth with us and want to enjoy the luxury of getting done what they have to do before we turn up to crowd and harass them and get in their way?

After a wait of only a few minutes more, but enough to

cause disgruntled muttering and overt glancing at watches, the doors were unlocked and opened, by another pimply youth who looked to John not unlike the misguided soul who had been on Bridges Junction station on Thursday evening. This lad, however, had obviously been schooled in customer care by his employer who realised that its customers had a choice where they shopped. Keeping calm, he welcomed everyone warmly to the store, as the grey panthers filed past him and dispersed among the shelves.

John strode in after them, heading resolutely for where he knew he would find the first item on his shopping list that day. On his weekly journey around the store he aimed to be focused, efficient and fast, working from a list of things he knew he needed, written down before he left home, in the order he knew he would find them. Of the other shoppers there that Saturday morning, some were like him in this respect and others were not. The former were no problem to him or anyone else: they knew what they wanted and where to find it. The latter dithered and dawdled, apparently confused by the amount of choice with which they were presented. His speed and precision were good, but not as good as they might have been had he not been hampered by the presence of these ditherers. As he sought to avoid them, his thoughts were invaded at regular intervals by a series of rhetorical questions, posed by the despairing voice of his inner self.

Why do other people always seem to stand, leave their trolleys, in front of the parts of the shelves I want to get to, he asked himself, when there are so many other places they could stop?

Will there ever be a place I can stand, when I do choose to stop, where I won't be in front of the shelves one of the ditherers then decides they want to reach? Why do some people find it necessary to turn their trolleys sideways across the aisle whenever they stop to pick something up from a shelf, thereby almost completely blocking it? It was a mystery to John how people could behave with such disregard for others; he had been brought up by his parents not to get in people's way, to go out of his way, in fact, to make sure he did not. The old could be excused, perhaps, by virtue of their age, but younger people had no excuse. John gritted his teeth and carried on.

The only redeeming feature was the absence so far of a particularly infuriating type of shopper: the ones who do not come into the store armed with a shopping list, or even with an idea of what they want to buy, but who conduct their tour of the aisles engrossed in a mobile phone call to someone else to find out what it is they need to buy. Because that someone else is not in the store and can have no idea where anything is, the result is a series of random move-ments, a kind of human equivalent of Brownian motion amongst gas particles, made without reference to anyone around them, because their attention is focused only on what is being said on the phone clapped to the side of their head. Nothing else, no-one else, anywhere else, is of any impor-tance to them. BOOM! John's imaginary elephant gun fires and the first imaginary mobile-phone-shopper of the day falls, their lifeless body and now-useless trolley coming to rest, as luck would have it, before the only empty section of shelving in the store, where neither will be in anyone's way any more. John takes an imaginary bow as everyone else in the store stops to applaud him loudly, before turning away to carry on with their shopping.

Back in the real world once more, John glanced to his right, along the aisle between the delicatessen and cheese counters, through the double doors at the head of the cor-ridor that ran back into the bowels of the back-of-house areas – doors that had been left wide open to allow goods to be pushed out on large-wheeled trolleys to replenish the stock on the shelves. He paused for a moment, his attention drawn by a raised voice coming from the far end of the corridor, and the sight of three men standing there in a group. Two of them, both older than John, were being given a sound telling-off by the third, who looked a lot younger. John stared, seeing in them a parallel with his situation at PLGC. The young man doing all the talking did not have a shaved head, bore no particular physical resemblance to the dreaded Roland, and was managing to express himself in measured language, without resorting to insults or profanity, but the parallel was in the situation: with older people placed in the power of the young.

Where and when, John asked himself, had it all gone wrong? When he was young it had seemed to him that the world was run by the wise old heads of generations of people older and more experienced than he was, and he had grown up with the unshakeable conviction that when he was older his generation would, in their turn, take up their rightful place at the head of things and assume control. Then, as time went by, he began to realise, with mounting horror, that the faces of the people who were making the important decisions in the world – the politicians, the style gurus, the leaders in every sense of the word – had suddenly become younger than he was. Somehow his generation seemed to have missed their opportunity to take control, and were now condemned to be mere followers for the rest of their lives. How had it happened? he asked himself again.

Sobered by what he had just seen, he hastened to complete his shopping before the arrival of more ditherers and the first real mobile-phone-shopper of the day.

Glad to have escaped into the sunshine and fresh air once more, John pushed his trolley, now loaded with his shopping packed neatly in the bags he had brought with him, to the taxi rank. Down on foot and back by taxi; that was his habit, as the loaded bags were too heavy for him to carry alone, and the security staff objected when shoppers tried to take their trolleys home. With the driver's help he transferred his bags from the trolley to the boot of the cab, then slid into its back seat and shut the door.

The taxis in Asham were generally driven during daylight hours by older men of the more sensible kind, either retired and in need of an income to supplement their pensions, or made redundant, mostly from middle management jobs, people allegedly found not to have been doing anything useful when the bright young things had taken the helm, people deemed to be too old, too set in their ways, too near retirement to make a useful contribution to the business from which they were ousted. This part of the country had what was probably the most over-qualified, literate and knowledgeable force of taxi drivers anywhere in the world. This was to the advantage of people like John, who were treated with civility and respect, and whose right to silence on their journeys was respected. If they wanted to talk, they were treated to a little intelligent conversation, rather than: 'Ere, guv'nor, you'll never believe 'oo I 'ad in the back o' me cab the uvver day, no' in a farzand years yer won't!'

Meanwhile, back in the businesses from which they had been ousted, staff were finding out the hard way what it was their former managers had been doing so well for so long that it had all been taken for granted and nobody had realised they were actually doing it; it was, of course, far from the nothing the bright young things had imagined it to be. Those unfortunates had no choice but to take over the tasks themselves, on top of their existing workloads, with no extra pay and no recognition for doing so. They were, in modern management-speak, 'empowered'.

Home again, with the bags of shopping placed on the dining room floor, just beside the doorway leading through to the kitchen, John started to unload his purchases into the cupboards and onto the shelves, in the fridge or freezer, wherever the items belonged. Once done, for the rest of the morning he attended to his housework, making the house as clean, neat and tidy as his parents would have expected to see it while they were still alive, for their values and virtues lived on in their son.

After lunch he spent the afternoon in his garden, in the battle he waged with nature every year. He was not a natural gardener, and struggled to make the small plot behind his house look anything more than barely presentable. He found it frustrating. The plants he wanted to grow steadfastly refused to prosper while the weeds flourished in profusion. His lawn was never anything more than a scruffy patch of grass, a long way removed from the lush, springy turf of a Wembley or a Wimbledon. He worked long and hard, but when he stood up at the end of the day and stretched the muscles in his aching back, he was not convinced he could see much for his efforts. With a sigh of resignation, he pulled off his gardening gloves, turned and went back into the house, to wash, change and prepare his dinner.

That evening John went to the cinema with his friend, Pete. This was another of his regular habits. It had begun in the days when they were both a lot younger and thought of themselves as likely-lads, going to a good place to 'pull the birds'. The 'birds' had proved elusive, and time had passed them by, making them first less likely-, then less than likely- and, finally, unlikely-lads. No longer likely and no longer lads, they now went along for the company, the films and a swift pint afterwards in The Pig and Truncheon. The dream of romance or an encounter with the seamier side of life had proved to be just that, something acted out by movie stars, creating the celluloid fantasies they watched each week. Saturday gone, Sunday beckoned, bringing Monday and his return to the clutches of the dreaded Roland a day closer.

Sleep eluded him for a long time that night, and he lay

on his back staring up into the darkness between him and his bedroom ceiling. The prospect of returning to work, to face Roland, hung heavily on his mind. He was, he knew, not good with interpersonal conflict – something that characters like Roland seemed to live and thrive on. John's aim was simply to get on with the work he had to do. He hoped people would think well of him at best, or just leave him to himself at worst. But Roland seemed to think that creating friction and conflict brought out the best, not only in himself, but in the people who worked under him.

Sleep came eventually, sometime in the early hours of the morning; not the deepest of sleeps admittedly, but relaxing and refreshing enough, and he woke up in a slightly more optimistic frame of mind than he had found himself in the day before. Roland would be in the office Monday morning and would, without doubt, be as abrasive and obnoxious as usual, but at least John had the prospect of working on the Perma-way project to look forward to. He had found it interesting and absorbing, and just for a moment he found himself fantasising that when he presented his work later in the week, Stephen Dent and his colleagues would be so pleased with what he had achieved they would offer him a job on the spot, taking him away from PLGC and Roland. Oh, blessed fantasy!

On that Sunday he had nothing special planned, so he spent the day finishing off. First he finished reading the paper from the day before, over a leisurely breakfast. Then he finished the housework by cleaning the bathroom and the kitchen, the sink, the worktops, the cooker and the floor. Then he went outside and finished the gardening he had started the day before, though what he had achieved at the end of it afforded him little pleasure. Finally he finished off his week's washing by ironing the clothes he had hung out to dry on his washing line earlier in the day, and while he ironed he watched an old Second World War film on the television. Then that day was gone too, and it was time to face the fact that the start of the working week was only a matter of hours away.

In the evening he sat in front of the television as he ate his ready-meal, a traditional roast dinner with all the trimmings. What he watched, as a means of escape, was a re-run of a two-hour long, made-for-TV detective story, set in a small country village where, week and week about, a significant proportion of the inhabitants was murdered, in a variety of inventive and gory ways. The detective always got his man, or woman, in the end, so everything turned out well – except for the nine or ten people who lost their lives before Detective Chief Inspector Slowbody managed to work out (or was told by his daughter) who was behind it all. John could not help but think that if such things were to happen in real life there would be widespread panic, a hue and cry, and a mass exodus from villages all over the country which not even calming words from the Home Secretary of the day would be able to arrest. Either that, or everyone living in the country would be dead within a few weeks. Suspending your disbelief for a while was all it took, though, to produce a good evening's entertainment and send you off to bed still chuckling at the thought of how ludicrous it all was.

Even though his evening was nominally at an end, John did not take himself straight up to bed. Instead he sat and watched another programme, one he had stumbled across on one of the BBC channels as he was idly channel-hopping before turning off the television. This was a programme in which a group of men, branded by the show's title as 'grumpy' and 'old' were eloquently presenting their views on what was wrong with life, the country and everything, and what should be done to put it right.

John could see that the point of this programme was to extract humour from what they said but, as far as John was concerned, they all talked such obvious and eminent sense, that any who disagreed should be held up to ridicule themselves. Here, he thought, are the people who should be in charge, not the bright young things with their half-baked ideas and convoluted, alienating language.

At the end of the programme, buoyed up by the realisation that he was clearly not alone in his beliefs, he retired to bed somewhat happier.

6

Week Two

On Monday afternoon John finished the Perma-way work, had the databases neatly compiled and loaded onto compact discs, along with a list of the references he had used as he assembled the information. Then he phoned Stephen Dent to set up the next meeting, which they agreed would be at two o'clock on the following afternoon.

At the appointed time he made his way to Overway House again. Approaching the glass doors from the station foyer, he recalled his embarrassment last time and the scornful attitude of the receptionist, so he went straight to the right-hand side, pushed hard on the glass of the door and walked straight into it with a resounding bang – it stayed resolutely shut. The receptionist looked up at the noise, saw John and smiled, but not in a pleasant way. Peering over the top of her fashionable glasses, she extended the exquisitely-manicured forefinger of her right hand, pointed it directly at John, then moved it slowly to the right to indicate that he should go to the revolving door in the centre of the glass wall. The slow, deliberate circling motion she then made with that finger told him that it was now working. He moved across, as instructed; he pushed; the door turned, swallowing him up and regurgitating him on the other side, inside the entrance hall.

'The doors have been fixed then,' he said as he approached the receptionist's desk.

'Evidently,' she responded

'John Biddle', he said. 'Come to attend a meeting with Stephen Dent.'

Once again she went through the routine of searching the typed list of expected visitors lying on the shelf in front of her.

'Executive floor, ' she told him. 'Take the lift on your left-hand side. You'll be met at the top.' As he walked away, he knew without having to look that he was being executed again, by another swift stroke of her pen.

This time, when the lift reached the top floor, he was not kept waiting at all. Irwin Lee was already there to meet him.

'John,' he said, extending his hand. 'Good to see you again.'

'And you,' John replied, taking the hand and shaking it.

'Come on through,' Lee said, leading him into the room where the previous meeting had been held. Stephen Dent was there, as was Bill Taylor, the Commercial Director, Gordon Harper, the IT Director, and Adrian of right arse fame. He greeted each in turn, and was then introduced by Irwin Lee to the one man in the room he had not seen before.

'John, this is Martin Adams. He's our Deputy IT Director. He couldn't be with us last time, but as it's his people who'll be handling the information you'll be providing us with, he's joining us today.'

John offered his hand to the man he was being introduced to.

'Ah, John,' Adams said. 'Nice to meet you. So you're our 'man beyond reason', are you?' He stopped short with a gasp as Irwin Lee nudged him sharply in the ribs.

John must have looked surprised, as the attacker quickly said, 'Take no notice of him. He had a bad experience with an actuary once; thinks they're all unreasonable people now.'

John was about to say that he was really an actuarial technician and not the real thing, but found himself being steered away by Lee.

'Cup of tea, John? Or coffee perhaps?' Lee asked him. 'We have a particularly fine Earl Grey over here you might like to try.'

Out of the corner of his eye, John saw Adams leaving the room, rubbing his sore ribs gingerly, and being propelled by Adrian Wright. John just caught the words, 'How was I to know if nobody tells me? No-one ever tells me anything around here...' as he went.

And what could that have been about? John wondered. He had no time to speculate; the meeting was called to order by Stephen Dent.

Everyone sat down around the table, with a laptop computer, connected to a projector.

'John tells me,' said Stephen Dent, 'that the task we set for him is complete, and he's brought the results with him today. So, it's over to you John – if you'd like to use the laptop there.'

John walked around the table, waited while Gordon Harper turned the machine on and made it ready, then loaded the first of his compact discs into the drawer on the side. At the click of the mouse the first database appeared on the wall. For the next hour or so, he presented his work to the small group of men clustered around the table, explaining the information, where it had all been collected and for what it might be used. He began slowly and nervously, but relaxed as he got into his subject and, after a while, was surprised to find that he was quite enjoying himself. Stephen Dent and his colleagues listened avidly. At the end of it John passed out a set of notes he had prepared as a summary guide to the content and use of each of the discs.

'I have to apologise for not being able to complete the very final stage of the project, which should have been to reduce everything I've shown you to a single baseline for direct comparison of all the figures. To do that I would have needed to get more detailed information on exposure times than I was able to find, but that doesn't appear to be easily available anywhere. I've written up what I think would be needed at the end of the notes so it can be picked up and continued at some time in the future if needs be.' Stephen Dent slid back in his chair, having leaned forward throughout John's presentation, concentrating hard on what was being said.

'You're to be congratulated, John. That's an excellent piece of work, which will, I think, suit our needs very well indeed. Do you agree, gentlemen?' he said, addressing his colleagues. They nodded their agreement. John removed the last of his discs from the laptop, slid it back into its protective case, then put them all into the waiting hand of Gordon Harper, the IT Director, whose staff would now be taking ownership of the information they contained. With that, the business part of the meeting was over. Pleasantries were exchanged for a short while and John was thanked again for his good work before everyone stood up, shook hands rather formally and said their goodbyes.

On leaving the room, John was escorted to the lift lobby by Stephen Dent, who, amid further expressions of gratitude, said that if anything more was needed he would be in touch. They were the only people in the lobby just then, except for the mysterious Adrian Wright, who had absented himself from the whole of the meeting. He was standing in one corner, talking to someone on a mobile phone as they entered, but he stopped speaking and appeared simply to be watching them as they waited for the lift to arrive. As the lift doors slid shut John observed Mr Wright, still looking steadily in his direction, begin to speak into his phone once again, leaving him with the distinct and uneasy impression that the conversation was, for some reason he could not begin to guess at, about him.

As the meeting had not taken very long and he still had work to do for Roland, and another leaving party to attend later, John went back to his office for the rest of the afternoon. From there he went to The Broker and Bitch with his colleagues, drank more than he probably should have done, then headed off towards the station, his bladder already beginning to fill.

The train he caught was a slow service, stopping at all stations to Asham, but long before he got there he would, he knew, have to go to the toilet to make himself more comfortable. Finding that the cubicle on board the train was out of order as a result of vandalism, he decided to get off at Bridges Junction, use the station toilet there, then take the semi-fast service to Smalltown via Asham which he knew would not be far behind.

Everything went to plan, and when he arrived on platform three at Bridges Junction to wait for the second train, feeling more comfortable and much happier, he could see from the destination board hanging from the rafters of the station canopy that he had a little over ten minutes to wait – no hardship on such a warm summer's evening as this.

As he waited he looked around at sights familiar to him to the point of boredom from his having seen them too often in the past, day in and day out on his journeys through the place every morning and evening. The only thing different was the construction site to the east of the station, where a new apartment block was being built: every day it was a little taller, a little bigger than it had been the day before. Even that quickly lost its appeal as he realised there was no work going on, the builders having finished for the day, leaving a motionless tower crane standing sentinel over the partly-completed, concrete skeleton of the building.

Looking around him again, now with nothing better to do, he began to play a game that he often indulged in when he was bored and could think of nothing more constructive to occupy his mind with when he was travelling. This game involved looking at his fellow passengers and trying to guess where they were going, just from observing their outward appearances. This was, he knew full well, a game that drew strongly on his innate prejudices, as it was entirely wrong to classify or judge people merely from their looks. It was quite possible, he knew, for a vegetarian pacifist, or even a Royal Prince, to go to a fancy dress party in the guise of Adolf Hitler or Rudolph Hess, but he also knew that it was highly unlikely that such a thing would happen. And there were easy precedents. People with large amounts of luggage were usually heading to or from the airport. Youngsters wearing hooded jackets and baseball caps, who spent their time stalking up and down the aisles shouting obscenities at each other, were almost invariably going to the huge indoor shopping centre in 'Sarfnew'un'.

Others were more difficult to guess, like the portly middle-aged man with short, greying hair and a moustache whom John found waiting on the platform when he emerged from the Gents. This man presented him with something of a mystery. John knew for certain that he had got off the earlier Asham train and was now, apparently, waiting for another one going in exactly the same direction. John had, of course, done exactly the same thing, but with a distinct purpose in mind. This man had not needed to go to the toilet, however, and seemed to have no obvious reason for his course of action. It was mysterious indeed!

Later, John would tell himself that he should have realised what was going on sooner because the clothes gave the man's secret away. But perhaps that was only something he realised with the benefit of hindsight. At the time, all he saw was a man, reasonably well turned-out, wearing shiny black shoes, dark grey trousers, a black blazer, white shirt and a tie with some kind of emblem or badge woven into it. By his side he carried a smart leather briefcase. Perhaps he was just another commuter, with some perfectly valid reason for changing trains at Bridges Junction. John decided to forget about it.

When the next train arrived, he walked along the platform towards its front end, got into the first of its four carriages and took a seat facing the back. The doors slid closed and the train moved off. At first there was no sign of the other man; then John realised he could be seen through the glass panels in the doors between the carriages, moving slowly forward along the aisle. John looked away quickly to stare at the passing countryside. When he ventured another glance along the aisle, he could see that the man had taken a seat not far away from the front of the next carriage, from where he could see John through the windows in the dividing doors and from where John could also see him. Suddenly, he became convinced that this man was following him.

Having reached this somewhat unlikely conclusion, and unable to shake off the idea, John decided to play a game to test his theory. As the train made its way through the countryside between Southnewtown and its next stop, at Smallholt, he got up and began to walk back along its length towards the toilet at the far end of the second carriage, past the man he now saw as his 'shadow'. But as he approached it he veered off to stand in the gap between the seats alongside the rear set of sliding doors, as though intending to get off at the next stop. There he stood until the train halted at Smallholt station. Looking forward along the carriage, he saw the other man get up and walk across to the front set of doors, as though he, too, intended to get off. The doors slid open. John turned and almost ran into the toilet cubicle which, fortunately for him, was not occupied at the time. He stayed there until the train had moved off again, travelled most of the distance between Smallholt and Asham, and was slowing down again. As it eased its way into Asham station, John slid back the bolt on the toilet door and walked out, along the aisle and through the opening doors. Out of the corner of his eye he saw his shadow doing the same thing.

John walked slowly up the steps onto the footbridge, knowing that the other man was only paces behind him, apparently oblivious of John's suspicions. They crossed the bridge and turned right onto the staircase leading to ground level again. On the landing, halfway down the stairs, John suddenly stopped and ducked down, as though stooping to tie a loose shoe lace. He waited until he could feel the bulk of the person behind looming over him, then stood up quickly, turning as he did, and charged head first into the stomach of his shadow. The man emitted a grunt and sat down heavily on the step behind him. His briefcase bounced noisily down the lower flight of concrete steps, landed with a clatter at the bottom and burst open. John, moving more quickly than he had for many years, bounded down the stairs to rescue the case. Gathering up its spilled contents, he remounted the stairs towards its owner, who was now on his feet again and had regained his composure.

'I'm so very sorry,' John said, handing him the now-closed case. 'I've just remembered something I need to get in town before I go home. It was my fault entirely. Are you OK?'

The man said that he was, and muttered something about being more careful in future. Then he had no option but to continue down the stairs, while John went back up and left him behind. To do anything else would have been to give himself away completely. He might have suspected, from John's unpredictable actions, that the game was already up, but he could not afford to take a chance.

John walked quickly back across the bridge, his mind in a whirl. He now knew for certain that he had been followed by a Mr Marlon Y. Large, employee of Amalgamated Risk Services (Europe) Limited. That, at least, was what it said on the business card he had taken from the briefcase before returning it to its hapless owner: Marlon Y. Large, Consultant: e-mail m_y_large@arse.com.

Later, as he sat in front of the television in his sitting room, having made his way home by a circuitous route without seeing again the man he now thought of as 'Large Arse', John's certainty about events on the trains that evening began to slip away and he decided that his being followed must be, could only be, a figment of his imagination. After all, why would anyone want to follow him? Then, during the darkest hours of the night, as he lay in his bed unable to sleep, he convinced himself that it was all too much of a coincidence that he should seem to have been tailed by someone who turned out to be working for Arse, when he had not even heard of such an organisation until his recent association with Perma-way. And that, he found, when day broke over the world again, was the more compelling interpretation of events.

On leaving the house that Wednesday morning, the world seemed to him a completely different place, an altogether darker and more threatening place. Where before there had merely been innocent people dotted along the route he took to the station – postmen, newspaper boys, people waiting for buses or lifts in friends' cars – now there were spies, watching his every move, ready to report back to Adrian Wright and his shadowy organisation. He carried his suspicions with him all the way to his office. On the train and on his walk through Suburbia to PLGC's building he was on the lookout for faces he recognised, that he would see more than once, whose owners might be following him, but there were too many people going in the same direction. He looked also for the tell-tale signs of an Arse man – the blazer, the dark trousers with their militarily precise creases, the regimental tie – but there was nothing of the kind to be seen anywhere.

Throughout the day he struggled to concentrate on his

work. Again and again, he found his mind wandering back to the events that preoccupied him. Eventually he gave up trying to work and submitted to the urge to wallow in his predicament. Making sure Roland was nowhere to be seen, he opened up the internet connection on his computer and typed the word 'Arse' into the search engine. This was, he knew, highly risky, as the company's employees were banned from using the internet for private purposes during working hours, and accessing the sort of websites likely to be reached by typing the word 'Arse' into company-owned equipment was probably an offence that would result in instant dismissal at any time. By then, however, he no longer cared. The cumulative effect of Roland's abuse, the tale about the book of railway stories and now the thought that he was being followed by one or more of Adrian Wright's men had served to change something inside him, something that would never be the same again.

John looked at the computer screen and contemplated the size of the task confronting him – the search engine had found nearly four and a half million websites across the world containing the word 'arse'. Deciding that he might have more luck if he used the company's full title, Amalgamated Risk Services (Europe), he entered that – but the search engine found nothing at all. Risking everything, he returned to the search for 'Arse' and began looking at the websites listed, one by one.

Hours passed as John sifted through the front pages of websites dedicated to sado-masochism, surgical procedures for reducing buttock sizes, or specialist clubs in seedy backstreets from Bangkok to Bigton. Several times he had to click hurriedly into a spreadsheet he also had open on his computer to avoid being observed by someone walking past, but none of those people was Roland, and none was at all interested in what he was doing. Then, just as he had decided to pack up and leave, he discovered something different, something unlike all the other websites he had so far vis-ited. He did not at first understand what he was looking at. On second reading it began to make some sort of sense. It was a story about some kind of military operation, carried out several years before by an American quasi-governmental security agency in one of the smaller independent African republics. The details were not important to John, but one line caught his eye, in which it stated unambiguously that the whole operation was based on intelligence information supplied to the Americans by an organisation called Arse.

John froze. When he set out to find out about Arse, he had not known what he expected to find, but he knew it was nothing like this. He shut down his computer, packed up his things and left, uncertain whether he would ever see that place again, as he now had no idea what lay ahead of him. A few days before, his destiny had seemed clear: a steady job, with a steady income up to the date of his retire-ment, then a reasonably good pension with which to pay for a reasonably comfortable old age. Now nothing was clear at all. He seemed to be some kind of marked man, stalked by the agents of what looked like a high-powered security agency. But why?

He travelled home that evening like an automaton, his mind numbed by the discovery he had made. He did not even register the face of Adrian Wright in the crowd on the station, even when the two of them momentarily stared directly at one another, nor the considerable delay his train suffered when someone barricaded himself (or herself) inside one of the toilets and insisted on smoking, thereby setting off the alarms and bringing the whole of the rush-hour in South Suburbia to a grinding halt. Nor did he remember hearing the guard's announcement: 'We'll be staying put here while the train crew batter the door down to get them out.' Only in the middle of the night, when he should have been soundly asleep but was, instead, resolutely awake, did the numbness begin to pass and his brain start to function again.

What, he asked himself, is the connection between me and Arse? The only possible answer was Perma-way, and the work he had been doing for them. But why would someone, anyone, want him watched just because he was working for them? Is it the nature of what I've been doing? I don't see how it could be. It's not exactly top-secret stuff, is it? No, it had to be something else. But what? He began to consider everything that had happened while he was inside Overway House, between his arrival there for the first meeting and the time of his exit after the second. He relived each moment in as much detail as he was able to recall.

All he could think of was the slightly odd incident, just before the start of the second meeting, when the newcomer, the Deputy IT Director, Adams, had said something strange, something that had led to his being escorted from the room by Adrian Wright, not to return. What was it he had said? Something about John? No. About actuaries in general being unreasonable? He struggled to remember the exact words. The phrase 'A man for all seasons' came to mind, but he knew it was not that. Then he had it. Adams had described him as 'Our man beyond reason', whatever that might mean. Then he had said something else, as Adrian Wright pulled him from the room.

'How was I to know if nobody tells me? No-one ever tells me anything around here.'

That was it. Those were the last words Adams spoke as he left the place. But what was he talking about? John lay on his back, staring up at the dark ceiling above him, looking for answers, but finding none. He was getting nowhere. He rolled over and tried to sleep, setting aside the events of the day, trying to make his mind a blank, so that his body could rest.

When he woke up it was daylight outside, and almost

time to get ready for work. But there was to be no work for him that day. His world and his understanding of it had now changed so much that there could be no going back, no more strict adherence to the humdrum routine that had hitherto been the stuff of his daily existence. He was now determined to find out what was going on, and why.

Sleep had sharpened his wits and helped to clarify some of the thoughts that, until then, had existed only in a confused jumble inside his head. He had realised that he was, for reasons he did not yet understand, at the centre of some kind of secret conspiracy involving Perma-way and the work he had done for them. Martin Adams, in speaking out of turn, had imparted to him some information or knowledge he was not supposed to have, the clue to what it was being contained in those two words 'beyond reason'. Whatever it was, Perma-way had obviously thought it valuable as they had hired an expensive security consultant to make sure it stayed secret. John, having heard those words, was now judged a security risk, and was being watched and followed; What else? he wondered; then shuddered at the thought of the thought he dared not think.

But what was he going to do about it all? Doing nothing was not a viable option; it left too much unanswered, too many uncertainties. Mulling over what he knew about secrets and conspiracies, knowledge gleaned mainly from the paperback thrillers he read on trains and the detective stories he liked to watch on TV, he knew that the most common motive for plotting and intrigue was money, and he saw no reason why that should not be the case here. It was obviously connected with more than health and safety records and advertising campaigns, and yet it must have something to do with the information he had compiled. Find and follow the money, he told himself, and everything else will fall into place. Quite how he was going to do that, he was not sure.

He got up and put on some of his oldest clothes – the

jeans he usually wore for gardening and a short-sleeved T-shirt in a dreary pastel shade that one of his elderly aunts had given him. Then he hunted down a wide-brimmed Panama hat from the back of his wardrobe, and got out his sunglasses. As disguises went it would not be particularly convincing but he hoped it would be enough. Leaving the curtains closed across the downstairs windows at the back of the house, he ate his breakfast, and waited for his neighbours to leave for work.

At just before ten o'clock he decided the coast would be clear and got up to leave. He checked his pockets to make sure he had everything he thought he would need. Then, carrying his hat and sunglasses, he left the house through the back door. Out in the yard he looked about warily, expecting to find the agents of Arse lurking everywhere – around the back corner of the house, behind his potting shed, wherever they could secrete themselves. There was no-one to be seen. One of the benefits of staying in the same place for a long time, amongst the same neighbours, was that you got to know a lot about the people who lived around you: where they worked, what time they left home each day, which of them looked after the boundaries around their properties and which of them did not. Luckily for John there were quite a few in that part of the town who were guilty of neglect in that respect, and he now made use of their laziness as he pushed his way through gaps between loosely-fixed fence panels and over low and broken-down walls, moving from garden to garden and house to house along the row. When he decided hc had gone far enough he stopped, put on the sunglasses and hat, strolled down the length of the garden he found himself in, to the gate at the bottom, and let himself out into the alleyway beyond it, trying as hard as he could to look as though he had every right in the world to be there.

Once in the alley he shut the garden gate behind him

and turned to walk towards the town centre, glancing around him casually. Away at the far end, a youth, dressed in a leather jacket, jeans and white trainers, was leaning against the woodwork of the last fence in the row, pulling on a cigarette. If he was an Arse man, this would be the test of John's disguise. Out of the corner of his eye John saw the youth straighten as he turned to walk away, then relax and re-assume his affectation of boredom, leaning against the wood behind him and idly blowing smoke into the air. John's ruse appeared to have worked: any pictures they had must have shown him in his working clothes, and the combination of his change of attire and his appearance in the alley through a gate so far down the row were enough to prevent him from being identified. Even then it was as much as he could do to stop himself running as he turned the corner into the street at the far end of the alley.

An advantage of living in the older part of the town, John found that morning, was the street layout: long, straight roads in a grid pattern, with lots of right-angled corners, made it easy to see whether or not the youth was following him. It was not so very long, and just a few corners more, before he knew that he was not. He headed south, towards the town centre, stopping long before he got there in front of a small row of shops where he knew there was a public phone box. With a final check to make sure he was still not being followed, he slipped inside, picked up the receiver and dialled the number of his friend Pete's mobile phone.

'Pete. Hi. It's John.'

'John. How're you doing?'

'Fine,' John told him, 'fine. Listen, Pete, are you at home at the moment? I need to ask a favour.'

'No. I'm at a client's office in London right now, doing a software fix. What do you need?'

'I need to look for something on the internet. It's something I can't do from work, and I'd rather do it without being spotted by anyone if I can.'

Pete knew straight away what John meant by that. Pete's work was not always strictly 'above board' and John knew that his friend had set up one of the computers in his workshop to be as near to undetectable on the internet as it was possible to be. From that computer, Pete's internet access and e-mails went to his carefully selected Internet Service Provider, where they were de-railed electronically and sent out again, from the ISP's central server, only its address being recorded as their point of origin. In that way the identity of the original sender or surfer was protected – unless the ISP chose to reveal it. Needless to say, they did not give up their secrets easily or lightly, as that was what their clients paid them for. That was the machine John wanted Pete to let him use.

'OK,' Pete told him. 'Go to my place and use my computer. You know which one. The key's where it usually is. I'll be back mid-afternoon. See you then?'

'Yeah. See you then. Thanks, Pete.'

John replaced the receiver. He knew that what he had just done might seem paranoid, but discovering the day before that Arse had links to organisations like the CIA had left him in something of a state of shock, and he was not about to take any chances by using phones that might be bugged or internet connections that might be monitored.

From the phone box he made his way to Pete's house, a spacious, nineteen-thirties semi-detached property, located in a tree-lined avenue on the western side of the town. As he walked, he continued to look about him at regular intervals, to satisfy himself, as far as he was able to, that he was not being followed. On arrival he went round to the back, reached over the top of the gate at the head of the side-alley to slide back the bolt, and let himself into the workshop at the back end of Pete's garage with the key that was kept on a ledge under the eaves of the roof. Once inside he locked the door behind him, stood at the window and stared down the length of the empty garden behind the house, feeling safe for the first time since he had realised he was being followed, a day and a half before.

Then he slid into the chair in front of the computer, switched it on and typed in the user-name and password Pete had given him on a previous occasion. Up came the home page. John typed 'The Permanent Way Agency' into its search engine and hit the 'enter' key. After a short wait and a single click of the mouse he was at Perma-way's home page, listening to the music that had played in their lift as he ascended to the Executive Floor. He turned the volume right down so he did not have to hear it any more. As with many websites, Perma-way's home page allowed its visitors access on two levels: as a public user, to view information anyone could look at, and to another section that was pass-word-protected, for authorised users only. The protected part was what John wanted to access.

The next step took him a long time to make, as he had known that it would, for it could only be done by painstaking work of trial and error. A message on the screen invited him to enter a user-name and password. Finding the password would be the difficult part as he had no idea what it was. The user-name would be easy: he already knew that Perma-way directors used their full names, simply typed – he had seen Gordon Harper type his into the laptop at the start of the second meeting.

He decided to use Stephen Dent's identity, reasoning that the Financial Director, of all the people he had met in Overway House, would be the least likely to spend time looking at the company's website, and knowing that if he chose the name of someone who was already using the system, his attempt to log in would automatically fail. He typed 'Stephen Dent' into the 'user-name' box on the log-in screen and began the search for the password. He started with the obvious – 'beyond reason' – knowing that it would almost certainly fail; it was too obvious to work. He followed it up with every possible combination of capitals and lower case letters in those two words, with and without the space between them. Nothing worked. So he moved on to more obscure ideas, still connected with the phrase 'beyond reason'. He tried 'Bond Reason', 'BondReason', 'bondreason', 'bondReason', 'B ond Reason', 'b ond Reason' and all the other combinations of letters and spaces he could think of. Again, none of them worked. He leaned back in the chair and stretched his arms out in front of him. The clue must be in that phrase 'beyond reason'. He was sure the Perma-way directors were using it as a prompt to remember the password – only not, he now knew, literally.

What, he asked himself, is beyond reason? The first thing he thought of was what Irwin Lee had said at the time, that actuaries were unreasonable, without reason. That led to another list of possibilities for him to try, but none of those worked either, and it took him several hours to work his way through them. He asked himself the same question again: 'What is beyond reason?' 'Madness' That did not work either, but instinct (or was it just blind hope?) told him he was on the right track and beginning to get closer. He let his mind run free for a while, playing a kind of word association game, scribbling the results down on a pad of paper Pete had left lying on the desk. After unsuccessfully trying a range of words associated with insanity, he followed another train of thought. This time he hit the proverbial jackpot. There was once, he knew, a pop group called Madness, who had sung a song – and this is where it began to get interesting – called 'One Step Beyond'. The connection felt right to him.

His next step was intuitive, perhaps even inspired, as he remembered thinking about late-running trains, mobile phone calls and men on the moon. One step beyond – one small step for man – a man called Armstrong, the first man to set foot on the moon. He reached out and typed 'Armstrong' into the password box and hit the 'enter' button. The Permaway home page dissolved as he stared at it, to be replaced by a blank screen, occupied only by a cartoon of an hour-glass – the sands of time ran on. John held his breath, gripping the arms of the chair tightly.

The sand ran down and out, the hour-glass disappeared and the screen momentarily went blank. Then it flickered bright white, as the computer found and opened up what John immediately recognised as a spreadsheet. He breathed out and smiled slowly, knowing he had arrived at the place he had been trying so hard to reach.

His eyes flicked rapidly over the neatly laid-out blocks of numbers and letters. He had found it. Now all he had to do was work out what it was, and what it meant. The best place to start was, he knew, in the top left-hand corner, where any labels there might be at the heads of the columns and the ends of the rows would meet one another. He scrolled across and up the page into the corner, realising, as block after block after block of text rolled across the screen in front of him, what a large spreadsheet this was and what a lot of information it must contain. Eventually he arrived where he wanted to be and began to study the headings and labels.

It was immediately clear that the first column contained dates – it was headed 'DMY': day, month, year – and the actual dates recorded gave him some idea of exactly how big this spreadsheet was. The first on the list was from a good few years before then, subsequent entries having been made, it appeared, at least every day since then and, often, many times a day.

John then moved his attention to the headings at the top of the rest of the columns. There were, he found, twenty-one of them, divided into groups by spaces inserted between some of the columns, each denoted by a set of three letters in capitals, the much-favoured three-letter-acronym, to identify the content of the particular column. If only they were all as easy to work out as 'DMY' had been, but many were far more obscure and difficult. Reading across the line, beyond the large gap that followed 'DMY' he found: 'RDU', 'STU', 'SSU', 'TDU', 'TAU', 'MDU', 'TEU', 'CCU', 'CLU', gap, 'RDD', 'STD', 'SSD', 'TDD', 'TAD', 'MDD', 'TED', 'CCD', 'CLD', gap, 'DPU', 'DPD', 'RPI'. He also found, by scrolling down the sheet, that its rows were divided into blocks by horizontal gaps – blank lines – with labels at the head of each and every block, inserted in the large gap between the columns of dates and the next full column in the table. These labels read' AMP', 'MDS', 'PMP' 'NTS' – more of the ubiquitous TLAs.

Having completed his preliminary inspection of what he had effectively managed to burgle his way into, John pushed his chair back, got up, and went to the window again. Outside it was still a sunny summer's day. Nothing moved within sight in Pete's garden. Some distance away, someone was cutting their lawn with an electric mower, but apart from that and an occasional burst of birdsong, no sound intruded on the quiet whirring of the ventilation fan in the back of the computer. Satisfied that he was quite alone, he sat down again and began to think about the information in the table.

Two of the columns contained station names, typed in plain English so any fool could read them. The stations listed wcre from all over the rail network in the south. The column headings, he quickly realised, gcnerally fell into one of two groups, ending with either 'U' or 'D', the same station names appearing in different places in both groups, but with their order reversed in the second. Although John would never have claimed to be a railway enthusiast – at least not in the way some people are, the ones who can be found standing on the ends of platforms at the London termini writing in their notebooks the serial number of every train – but he did know enough to realise that, with the same station names appearing the way they did under the two headings SSU and SSD, it was likely that 'U' meant 'up', 'D' meant 'down' and 'SS' meant 'station-stop'.

Railway terminology sounds, and always has sounded, rather quaint to the ears of the layman. The use of the terms 'up' and 'down' is a case in point. Those two words are used to denote the direction in which a train is travelling, 'up' meaning travelling towards London and 'down' meaning away from it. This is all very well, but it assumes, first, that the observer knows which way London is, and, second, the train or track in question is actually running towards or away from London, which many lines across the country are not.

The term 'station-stop' is another interesting piece of railway terminology. Its origins are post-privatisation and are rooted in the application of political correctness to railway 'customer service' announcements. In the good old days, when people appeared to have more common sense than they do today, if anyone chose to get off a train when it stopped temporarily at a signal in the middle of the countryside and broke their heads, or fell from a speeding train and did likewise, it was ascribed either to bad luck or to their own stupid fault. Now such people are likely to sue the railway company and are often awarded substantial sums of money in compensation. There is no such thing as an accident; it is always somebody else's fault. So it was decided that guards could no longer say either 'The next stop on this service is such and such a station', because the train might need to stop at a signal in the middle of the countryside beforehand and someone, thinking it was the station they had just been told about, might try to get out, and break their head by doing so, or 'The next station on this service is whatever it might be', because the next station it passed through might be one at which the train was not scheduled to stop and someone, thinking they were missing their stop, might try to get out while the train was still travelling at speed and break their head. So the concept of the 'station-stop' was invented: a station at which the train is intended to stop. It is neither a stop somewhere other than in a station, nor a station at which the train is not intended to stop – a masterpiece of politically-correct English, and a statement of the bleeding obvious!

The table, John now knew, was split into two parts, one dealing with the 'up' lines and the other with the 'down', and it listed stations at which trains were expected to stop. The next pairs of columns contained figures that looked as though they might be times, as times are written in the format of the twenty-four hour clock. The first figure was invariably earlier than the second, in most cases by a matter of just a few minutes, but sometimes by a much bigger margin. That led him to the idea that 'TD' might be 'Time Due' and 'TA' might be 'Time Arrived' or 'Time Actual', the suffix 'U' or 'D' attached according to the direction the particular train was travelling in. Realising this also led him to the conclusion that the groups into which the rows in the table were bunched had something to do with the time of day: early morning – AMP – 'am peak'?; late morning – MDS – 'mid-day section or sector'?; afternoon – PMP – 'pm peak'?; evening – NTS – 'night-time sector'?, perhaps. The times that were listed in the columns on the right of each of those labels seemed to bear out this conclusion.

After 'TD' and 'TA', the 'MD' columns appeared to contain the differences between the other two, expressed in minutes – 'minutes difference'. Beyond that, it became much harder; 'TE', 'CC', 'CL', 'RD' and 'ST' had for John no obvious meaning. These columns contained sets of apparently meaningless numbers, except for 'CL', which had letters, usually 'BJ', or, in a few places 'N'. At the far end of each row, 'DPU', 'DPD' and 'RPI' seemed to be summaries of some kind. The numbers suggested a financial format and seemed to have been added up on separate lines at the end of each section of the day for which numbers had been entered on the other lines.

John was so lost in his thoughts that he failed to hear the latch click on the gate at the head of the path, nor the soft pad of footsteps on the surface of the concrete. A dark shadow fell across the surface of the desk and a hand rattled the door handle. He jumped and looked round to see Pete staring in at the window, and, with animated gestures, demanding to know why he was locked out of his own property.

'Sorry about that,' John said after he had let him in. 'Force of habit, I suppose, after a lifetime of keeping everything locked up.' It was a lie, of course, but Pete was not to know it. John's parents had been cautious and careful and believed in locking things up securely, and John had been ribbed in the past for having come out of the same mould.

'What are you up to then, my sly old friend?' Pete asked him, looking with interest at the computer screen. 'That doesn't look particularly interesting. I was hoping for something a bit spicier. That just looks like a dusty old spreadsheet.'

'It is a spreadsheet,' John told him, 'and, if you don't mind, I'd rather not tell you about it at the moment.'

'As you wish. I'm the last one to pry – unless it's something that looks particularly worth prying into, which, I must say, that doesn't. You carry on. I'll be in the kitchen getting us both a drink. If you need any help, just give me a shout.'

Pete disappeared into the house, leaving the door to the garage open behind him. John heard him moving about in the kitchen as he dug two cold bottles of lager out of the fridge and took their lids off. He brought one out to John, then went back inside the house, where, John could soon hear, he had settled down to watch a cricket match on the television.

John returned his attention to the screen and looked again at the last sets of letters and figures. The only thing that came to mind immediately was that 'RPI' normally meant 'Retail Price Index', but he knew that could not be right in this context; it must mean something else here. Then an idea occurred to him. He tested it with some simple arithmetic. Scribbling down some of the figures that he knew were associated with the length of time trains were delayed, he had soon proved, by doing some rudimentary calculations, that there was a simple relationship between those delays and the figures in the 'DP' columns. 'D' therefore meant 'Delay', and 'P' was, he thought, most likely to be 'Penalty'.

Scrolling back across to the left, he began to consider again the columns whose headings he had not yet identified. The numbers in the first of them all had two digits. In theory they could therefore lie anywhere between 01 and 99, but in practice he could see that they only went up to just over fifty. Something about them seemed familiar. He scrolled down the page, searching for something in one of the other columns that would help him discover what these numbers might represent. It took him several minutes to work it out, and when he did he laughed because it was so obvious. As he ran down the columns of data he began to see that the numbers tied up with groups of stations listed in the 'SS' columns – always the same numbers for the same groups of stations. These were the numbered routes the trains ran on. 'RD' stood for 'Route Designation', a fact he confirmed by looking for a record of a train running through Asham to London, and another running from London to the coast through Asham, the numbers of which he knew very well through having seen them displayed prominently on the trains he took every day to and from work.

The other column headings remained a mystery to him. The columns labelled 'ST' seemed to contain a limited range of entries, some just numbers, others a combination of numbers and letters. Under the heading 'TE', the entries were just numbers, ranging from single digits to several thousands, but no higher. The 'CC' entries comprised more numbers, from fifty-something to many hundreds, with a lot of repetition, but no discernible pattern, apart from a noticeable progression towards the higher numbers as time passed.

John leant back in his chair and drank his lager. It was time to take stock of what he had learned, as he doubted he would make any more progress simply by studying the column headings he had not yet identified. What he was looking at, he told himself, was a huge table, summarising the delays suffered by trains running on Perma-way's southern regional network on a day-by-day basis over a number of years; also summarising, in the columns on its right-hand side, the cost of those delays in terms of penalties levied, presumably by OFFTOS. But there was something more to it than that. There had to be, or the table would have ended with the 'DPU' and 'DPD' columns, where the 'Delay Penalties' were written down and added up. If it was nothing more, the 'RPI' column would not have been there, and nor would the last figure presented for each day and each section of each day, which John could see was obtained by subtracting the sum of all the 'DP' figures for any given period of time from the sum of the 'RPI' figures for the same period. The numbers obtained by doing this were either positive or negative, depending on whether the 'RPI' figure was bigger or smaller than the corresponding 'DP' figure. This, John knew, was the classic form of presentation for a balance sheet, where income and expenditure were combined to show profits and losses.

It was easy to see where the losses came from; the 'Delay Penalties' were all losses, pure and simple. But where did the income come from? The railway companies obviously derived income from ticket sales, but that could not be the money listed in the 'RPI' column of the table. To begin with, the figures listed were too small, and, secondly, that money was more than swallowed up by running costs, salaries, maintenance costs and all the other expenses incurred in the operation of the railway system, leaving the Government to make up the shortfall in subsidies to the companies involved. No, it was not that: this was all about income and expenses associated somehow with delays. What this table seemed to be telling him, judging from the fact that most of the final figures for each section of each day were positive, was that Perma-way were somehow making profits from the fact that the trains were being delayed; if that really was the case, it gave them a huge incentive to make sure that the trains were delayed as often as possible. How they could be doing such a thing he had no idea, but if he were right it would be a secret worth keeping, and going to great lengths to keep, and could well be the reason why Arse had become involved in it all.

But how did any of that explain his involvement, and the position he now found himself in? It doesn't, he told himself. There's even more to it than that, something I don't yet know, but something I'm going to have to find out.

He stared intently at the computer screen, going over and over the ground he had already covered. Outside, the late afternoon wore on into early evening, the bright sunlight of the day gradually turned to a more mellow light, and the shadows of the trees along the side of the garden began to stretch themselves out across the lawn. In the house, Pete stirred as the cricketers filed off the pitch and into the pavilion for their tea.

'Are you hungry, mate?' he asked, emerging through the door into the workshop.

'Do you know, I think I am,' John told him, pushing his

chair back, stretching out and yawning. 'What did you have in mind?'

'On tonight's gourmet menu we have the choice of fry-up, chips and beans, or pizza, chips and beans, each one accompanied by generous helpings of vintage ketchup, and a fine example of premium bottled lager. Which would you prefer, sir?'

'Pizza, I think, if that's OK with you.'

'It certainly is. Your wish is my command,' Pete replied. 'I will now retire to the kitchen to practise my culinary skills. How's the spreadsheet going?'

'I'm not exactly sure,' John said slowly. 'I think I've found out some of what I was looking for, but I still haven't got everything I need.'

'If you want some help, just let me know.'

'Actually, there is one thing. If I wanted to print this out, would I be able to?'

'I don't see why not, but let's have a look,' Pete said, leaning over his friend's shoulder and taking charge of the mouse. 'Wow, that's quite some spreadsheet you've got there,' he observed as he scrolled up, down and across it. 'It'd take some time and quite a lot of paper, and you'd end up with a huge jigsaw to look at. Do you like jigsaws?'

'I'll pay you for the paper, if that's a problem.'

'No need. I've got loads. My clients give it to me, even if they don't always know it. Do you want to print it now?'

'Not right now, but can you show me how?'

'OK', Pete said – and he did.

During the meal, they watched a DVD of Billy Connolly and John asked another favour of Pete.

'Would it be OK if I stayed here for a couple of days?'

Pete looked up in surprise.

'I don't see why not,' he said. 'Is there any particular reason, or have you suddenly developed a strong liking for my company?'

'I just need to be away from the house for a while.'

'Is this something to do with your mysterious spreadsheet?'

'I'd rather not say. Not right now.'

'You realise, of course, that I'm desperate to find out what you're up to, but I do respect your desire for secrecy. Your actions are beginning to intrigue me, Mr Biddle. If I didn't know any better, I'd say you're acting like I do when I'm up to something I shouldn't be.'

That night John stayed in Pete's spare bedroom, and lay on his back staring at the dark ceiling. The feel and sounds of the house were alien to him and kept him awake for a long time: that and the pendulum swinging from side to side in his head, first telling him that he was mad and his suspicions a product of an over-active imagination, then swinging back to confirm that it was all real and his fears were justified.

In the morning, Pete had another appointment to go to, this one in Bigton, and told John he would be back in the late afternoon. Pete worried about his friend as he drove away – John looked pale, tired and drawn. He wanted to be able to help him, but until John decided to tell him what this was all about, there was little he could do.

John spent the day printing the spreadsheet and working out how the jigsaw he had managed to produce fitted together. He carefully labelled each sheet of paper in the thick pile he had produced so that he could put them together in the correct sequence and follow the information they contained. After that, he went back to thinking.

7

Weekend Two

In the middle of Saturday morning, John left Pete's house and walked to Smallholt Station, where he boarded the first train heading up the line, towards London. He stayed on it until Bridges Junction, where he got off, walked down the ramp between platforms one and two, turned left at the bottom and left the station through its front entrance. Once outside, he followed the footpath on his right, around the open forecourt area where the taxis and buses stopped, then passed under the bridge that carried the railway tracks and the northern end of the station platforms over the road, and made his way towards the marketing suite built into the high wooden fence which surrounded the site of the apartment block being built along the station's eastern side.

After Pete had left for Bigton the day before and he had printed and collated the pages of the spreadsheet, John had sat still and stared hard at the vast collection of numbers and letters on the computer's screen. He had stayed there for most of what remained of the day, studying it. He concluded that the letters 'BJ' in the columns headed 'CL' must refer to Bridges Junction. More thinking followed and, after a successful search of the house for copies of the local paper and the yellow pages, and having made a phone call to one of the places he now wanted to visit, he had a firm plan established in his mind.

The marketing suite had been open for some time when John walked in, but he was still their first customer of the day. That was a disappointment as he had hoped he could find what he was looking for and slip out unchallenged, if not unobserved. That was clearly not the way it was going to be.

'Good morning, sir.'

He was greeted with a cheery smile by one of the two young women who staffed the place, as she rose from behind her desk and walked towards him. She was tall, blonde and businesslike. Her name badge proclaimed her to be Claire.

'Oh, good morning,' John muttered, gathering his wits and hastily reformulating his plans. 'I'm . . . er . . . I'm looking for a new flat. I spotted this place from the train and thought I'd stop off for a look around. Handy for the station . . . for trains . . . to London.'

'Well let me show you around,' Claire said. 'All the details you need to look at are here: layouts, floor plans, artists' impressions and prices; and when you've seen all you need, I can take you to view the show flat.'

Claire led him around the inside of the marketing suite, showing him the display boards mounted on the walls, pointing out the details. Finally, she took him to a display case in the centre of the room, where there was an architectural model of the block as it would appear when it was finished, including its surroundings: the road, the railway, the station and its associated buildings. This was more than John had been hoping for.

'If I leave you to look around on your own for a while,' Claire said, 'you can come and fetch me when you're ready and I'll take you round the show flat.'

'Thanks,' John said, thinking the attention she was paying him was so much more than he had wanted or planned for, but that he might as well take the time to find out as much as he could while he was there.

He stood in front of the model for a long time when she had gone, shifting his vantage point from time to time, looking at the miniature building and its surroundings from all angles. Then he moved slowly around the inside of the walls again, looking carefully at the plans and layouts, trying hard to memorise what they were telling him. When he left he had achieved his aim and was quite pleased with himself. True to her word, Claire had opened up the show flat, located on the ground floor of the new building just behind the marketing suite, and given him a guided tour. He made what he thought were appropriately appreciative noises.

'What do you think, then?' she asked him when the tour was over. 'Do you like what you've seen?'

'Yes, very much,' he told her. 'Do you have any brochures, showing the plans and layouts so that I can try to work out which type of apartment might be the best one for me to choose? I'd like to spend some time making sure I make the right choice.'

'Yes, of course,' she said, smiling, and produced a glossy-looking booklet containing everything he needed to know. Most importantly, there was a full set of floor and apartment plans for him to pore over at his leisure.

'Is there anything else I can help you with just now?' she asked.

' You'll probably think it's a bit silly really, and I'm sure everything's OK. It's just that a friend of mine bought a flat in a block like this a while ago. He sold his house and had to leave it on the day the flat should have been ready, but some vandals got into the building and damaged it, so it wasn't ready, and he didn't have anywhere to live for a while.'

'Oh, you don't need to worry yourself on that score, sir. We have a very good security company who take care of all that for us. We haven't had any problems of that sort here, and we don't expect to.'

'Are they on site all the time, then?'

'No,' she replied slowly. 'When the builders are working, the site managers look after it. When it's closed, the security company makes visits from time to time to patrol it. We haven't had any break-ins, vandalism or thefts so far.'

He told Claire he was very interested, but would have to think carefully as it would be a big investment for him to make and that he would be in touch when he was ready to take things further. Then he left and set off to walk around the perimeter of the site, outside the fence-line, on the pretext of taking one last look. When he was satisfied that he had seen all there was to be seen, he walked back to the station and waited for another train heading north. This time his destination was the small station known as The Boltons, two stops up the line.

The old, four-carriage, slam-door train rattled and shook its way along the track, stopping at the airport first. Here the platforms were strangely deserted – devoid of commuters, as they always were at the weekend, but also unusually empty of tourists. The leering face of Roamer-Phone was still there on the bill-boards, looking even bigger and more threatening when viewed across the deserted platforms than as a backdrop to the customary hustle and bustle. Then the train moved off and the face was gone.

Ten minutes later they arrived at The Boltons and John got off. He walked along the platform on his own, the only one to alight there; this was not a busy place even in the weekday rush-hours, at weekends it was quite dead. He left the station through the unmanned gate and walked down the ramp to the road. At the bottom he turned left along the deserted street, flanked on either side by neat, detached bungalows nestling in neatly-kept gardens tended by neat, retired couples, towards the main road running north towards London from Southnewtown, roughly parallel to the railway line. As he walked, the sound of birdsong was gradually replaced by the roar of traffic on the road ahead of him.

When he reached it he turned right and walked on for about fifty yards to a shop, set back from the footpath at the northern end of a row which housed the sorts of establishment found in similar suburban settings the length and breadth of the country. On the corner, behind the bright red post-box that stands guard on every such corner, there was a newsagent-tobacconist-confectioner. Then there was an insurance broker's, a hardware store, a convenience store, a bookie, an estate agent with a solicitor's office above it on the first floor, the ubiquitous Indian take-away, a tile shop and, finally, the place John had come to visit: The Boltons Army Surplus Store.

It had everything he had decided he would need – and a lot more besides. He worked his way slowly around the shelves and racks of clothing, weapons of varying kinds, telescopes, binoculars, torches, sleeping bags, boots, gas masks, gloves, climbing gear, diving gear, flying helmets, cameras, surveillance gear – anything and everything needed to equip a small revolutionary army, apart from jeeps and tanks. John bought a pair of black trousers, a black, roll-neck jumper, a pair of black trainers, a black balaclava ski-mask that would cover his whole head, leaving just slits for his eyes, nostrils and mouth, a pair of black gloves, a wristwatch with a luminous dial – as used (allegedly) by the SAS, a small but powerful torch and a neat pair of night-vision glasses. He paid for it all with his credit card, as he had no cash with him, put everything in the anonymous plastic carrier bag the man behind the counter gave him, then set out on his return journey to Pete's house.

His trip back was uneventful, but he still took the precaution of looking behind him from time to time on his way back to the house from the station, just to make sure he was not being followed. As he walked into the kitchen from the garage workshop, Pete came in through the other door, bleary-eyed and dopey, having only just got up.

'Hi, mate!,' he said cheerily on seeing John. 'Been out?'

'Yeah, I had some shopping to do.'

'What did you get? Anything interesting?' He reached out quickly and snatched the bag from John's grasp, opened it and peered inside. 'Yes, you did, didn't you, you sly old bugger! What's all this for, then?' he asked, a wicked grin spreading slowly across his face. 'I assume it's got something to do with your mysterious spreadsheet, or are you just turning yourself into a high-tech peeping Tom? Come on, what is it you're up to? Industrial espionage, I'll bet, you dark horse you.'

'I suppose I owe you some kind of an explanation,' John said, retrieving the bag and putting it down on the kitchen table. 'The truth is I don't really know what I'm doing – not yet, anyway. Something's happened and I'm not exactly sure what it is: but I mean to find out, and that's what this is all for.' He indicated the bag. 'I think it could be dangerous, so I'd rather not tell you any more right now, but I will do if I find I need to. I'll try to make sure it doesn't affect you, and I promise I'll warn you if I find what I'm doing puts you or this place in danger.'

'You really should tell me you know, in case it's illegal – in which case I ought to report it to the appropriate authorities – or in case I can help.'

'You're a fine one to talk about breaking the law,' John retorted. 'What exactly is it you do for a living?'

'I help people with their computer problems,' Pete said defensively.

'You mean you help people out with the problems they're having with *other people's* computers.'

'I don't know how you can say something so slanderous – or is it libellous? I never did learn which one was which.'

John stayed silent for a while, and Pete set about making his breakfast. As the eggs and bacon sizzled in the frying pan, John made up his mind to ask for the favour he needed.

'Will it be all right if I use your car tonight, Pete?' he asked.

'I should think so. What time do you need it?'

'Late,' John told him. There's somewhere I need to go after the trains and buses have stopped running.

'Be careful,' Pete warned, and grinned.

At midnight, John changed into the black clothes he had bought earlier, putting the balaclava ski-mask, torch and night-vision glasses into a small canvas bag he had found in the garage. He went downstairs to where Pete was waiting, the latter having deliberately stayed in all evening out of curiosity.

'Good God!,' he exclaimed. 'It's the Milk Tray man. And all because, the lady loves an actuary from Asham.'

'Shut up.'

'Seriously, John, be careful. I'm not sure you're cut out to be James Bond.'

'Neither am I,' John shot over his shoulder as he headed down the hall towards the front door.

John drove to Bridges Junction and parked the car in a side-street a short way to the east of the building site. He got out and closed the door quietly, leaving it unlocked, in case he needed to get back into it in a hurry, then stood still, listening to the quiet of the night. Back on the main road an occasional car drove past. No one was about; the local residents all seemed to have retired to their beds. Carrying the canvas bag, he made his way down to the main road, then turned left towards the railway bridge and the building site.

Both the site and the road running along the side of it were in darkness, the bulk of the concrete frame looming over the plywood panels of the high fence, its tower crane projecting skywards, the white-painted lattice framework of its mast and jib lit up faintly from underneath by the light which spilled upwards from the station. John turned left when he reached the fence and walked along in its shadow, heading for the place where he knew a dark green phone company cabinet stood on the footpath, its back hard up against the fence. That was where he planned to climb over.

When he got to the cabinet he crouched down beside it, pulled the balaclava and gloves out of the bag and put them on. Then he hung the glasses around his neck by their carrying strap, put the torch in his pocket and dropped the bag on the ground at the foot of the fence: it was dispensable and its job was done. He clambered onto the cabinet and peered over the fence, pausing only long enough to be able to see that the ground inside was clear of obstacles. Then he hoisted himself up and rolled over the top of the fence.

His landing on the other side was not a thing of elegance or grace, but was at least a soft one – he landed flat on his back in a puddle of liquid mud. Cold and wet, wondering why on earth he was doing this, while all the time enjoying the sense of adventure – the feeling that, at last, after all these years, he had actually come to life – he got up and walked quickly towards the building.

Within the confines of the unfinished apartment block it was very dark, but was at least sheltered from outside view, so John took the tiny torch out of his pocket and turned it on to light his way, but still he shaded its bulb with his hand so it gave out only as much light as he actually needed – there was no point in taking unnecessary chances. Following the route he had memorised from the floor plans, he skirted around piles of unused materials and rubbish until he reached the stairs; he slowly climbed up the four floors to what was currently the top. Extinguishing the torch, he picked his way carefully through the renewed darkness towards the tower crane.

The mast of the crane soared into the night sky above John's head, looking far taller and more daunting at close quarters than ever it had from a distance. He had never had much of a head for heights, and climbing the vertical steel ladder to the driver's cab promised to be the greatest challenge he had ever faced. With a determination he had not known he possessed, he stepped out onto the cold, steel rungs, grabbed the rails on each side of the ladder and started to climb; slowly, carefully, moving only one foot or one hand at a time, making absolutely sure he did not lose his grip.

When he reached the top, his legs like lead and his heart pounding, partly through effort, partly through fear, he stepped onto a tiny, steel-floored landing at the back of the cab. Daring to look down for the first time since he had started climbing, he could see the world spread out below him, looking smaller and more distant than he had imagined it would. He could see for a long way in all directions: to the lights of the airport to the north: over the orderly ranks of houses to the south and east; and, more importantly, down on the station and into the compound around the control room immediately to his west. He opened the door of the cab, went in and slid into the driver's seat. Lifting his night-vision glasses to his eyes, he looked into the compound below him, at the area behind its high fences, and his night's vigil began. Time passed slowly as John watched the comings and goings below. He had arrived in the driver's cab at about 1:30 in the morning, and stayed there for almost the next two hours. The last train passed through the station, heading south on its way to Bigton, at about 1:45 a.m. Fifteen minutes later, the last few staff members left the control room, got into their cars and drove away into the night. The compound was locked up from the outside by a man who, John guessed, was a security guard; he then walked back to the rear entrance of the station and disappeared inside. All remained quiet for a little over half an hour, at which point the man reappeared, walked up to the compound gates, opened one, let himself inside and closed it behind him. For ten minutes or so he walked around inside and outside the building, carrying out his scheduled inspection. Then he retreated inside the station, to stay out of sight for another half an hour or so, when he reappeared and did the same thing all over again.

John decided that he had seen everything he needed to; it was time for him to leave. He stood up, backed out through the door of the cab onto the tiny landing and started down the ladder, trying hard not to look down as he went. Behind him, out of his line of sight owing to the position of the ladder, a pair of bright headlights appeared on the road running past the site. The van they belonged to swung into the road alongside the fence and stopped outside the locked gates. The lights were extinguished. A large man emerged, a man wearing the uniform of a security guard and carrying a powerful torch. He went round to the back of his van, opened the double doors and let out a large dog, holding it firmly on a short leash.

John stepped off the ladder onto the uppermost concrete floor slab. The guard released the padlock that held the gates shut and pulled the chain free with one hand. The dog was now pulling hard against its restraint, eager to be let free to run around the site, which it saw as one of its many playgrounds.

John walked across the floor slab towards the head of the staircase. It was then he heard the guard slide the chain through the metal handles on the gates. He knew immediately what that sound meant, and that he was no longer alone or safe in the place. He snapped off his torch and continued walking towards the head of the stairs in the dark. Just short of the first step down, his foot made contact with a metal can and sent it rolling across the concrete and down the first flight of stairs with a noise that, in the still of the night, sounded deafening. John swore and froze.

Outside the gates the dog heard the noise. It pricked up

its ears and pulled harder on the leash, more eager then ever to be free, to find out what was going on. The guard, with his diminished powers of hearing – thanks mainly to the many years he had formerly spent working as a security assistant in some of London's noisiest nightclubs – heard nothing.

John stayed motionless, waiting to find out what would happen next, unaware of the dog's presence. As the gates swung open, the guard released the animal. It was off like a shot, bounding away into the darkness with a single yelp. John heard it and broke out into a cold sweat.

How the hell did I get myself into all this? he asked himself as panic rose within him. More importantly, how do I get myself out of it?

The dog made straight for the staircase.

John heard it coming, its paws thumping heavily on the concrete steps and its loud panting amplified by the hard surfaces of the walls as it rushed up towards him. In desperation he turned and ran. He had no idea where he was going, but the thought of his flesh being mauled by the slavering monster he imagined was racing towards him was more than enough to spur him into action. The dog knew with some certainty where it was going, but John had no idea, everything he had learned about the layout of the site lost in the whirlwind of his panic.

When the dog arrived at the top of the stairs, John was about two thirds of the way across the floor; between the head of the staircase and the handrail he realised must run around the edge of it. Swerving violently to avoid barely-seen pieces of timber, scaffold poles and other paraphernalia, he searched desperately for a way out. His first thought was that he should have run back to the crane and started back up the ladder, but realised almost immediately that doing so would have left him trapped. Should he jump off, or vault over the railings and try to climb down the outside of the building on the scaffolding that surrounded it?

The dog, working from a combination of training and instinct, took a different route, trying to cut off its prey as soon as it could. Its speed and agility proved superior and, as John approached the railing around the edge of the building, it emerged from behind a stack of bricks a short distance behind his left shoulder. Having clear sight of him, it made ready to pounce.

Now within touching distance of the railings at the edge of the floor, John's courage failed him and, instead of vaulting over and taking his chances, he tried to change direction. He swerved, his feet slipped out from under him, and the dog lunged. John careered across the scaffold boards, under the lower guard-rail, and fell feet-first into the tubular plastic rubbish chute that led away down the side of the building to a skip at ground level. The dog, having launched itself at his upper back just as he slipped, sailed straight over the top of him, over the scaffolding, over the upper guard rail, and out into the darkness beyond it.

Down in the small street that ran along the side of the building site all was quiet. The van stood on its own by the gates, the guard having followed his dog inside. The only person to be seen was an old man, out for a walk with his little dog, a timid animal that had recently developed a strange aversion to daylight and would now only allow its owner to take it out of the house for exercise in the middle of the night. The peace of their nocturnal stroll was suddenly shattered by two loud noises that came, almost simultaneously, from the building site on their left. The first was a thump and an extended, but muffled, cry of 'Oh shiiiiiiiiiiit!' followed by the sound of something heavy slithering down the rubbish chute. The second was the loud yelp of a large, airborne dog.

The chute continued to vibrate and rattle until whatever was inside it was deposited in the skip, whereupon a cloud of white dust was thrown into the air. It drifted over the boundary fence into the road a short way ahead of the man and his dog.

All of that they barely saw, however. Of more concern to them was where the flying dog, which appeared to be heading directly towards them, would land. Having leapt with all its might and energy at John's back and head, its yelp turned into a terrified howl as it missed its intended target, sailed out over the guard-rail on the edge of the floor and began to fall. Exactly what passed through its mind during its descent that night, no-one will ever know. Its life may have flashed before its eyes, as is supposed to be the case with humans in a similar position. It may have thought its lot was up but if it did, it would have been wrong, because it belly-flopped heavily into an open-topped water tank standing against the inside of the fence. Its landing threw a minor tidal wave out over the top, soaking to the skin the old man and half-drowning his poor little dog, which never got over the shock of the experience and from that day forward refused to venture out of the house altogether.

John, coughing and spluttering, covered from head to toe in the fine white dust, stood up slowly, glad to be alive after his fall, and grateful that the dog had not slithered down the chute behind him. Keen to get away as quickly as possible, he waded through the rubbish in the skip, then jumped directly from it, onto the top of the fence and down to the pavement on the other side. His landing was a heavy one but was as nothing compared to what he might have suffered if the dog, which he assumed he had left behind on the top floor of the building, had managed to get hold of him. He looked down towards the main road, where the guard's van stood, unoccupied. Then he turned and looked in the other direction. An old man squelched past, muttering angrily under his breath and pulling behind him a drowned rat on a piece of string. John stared in disbelief and the old man glared back.

How on earth, John wondered, does an old man, pulling a rat, come to be soaked to the skin on a warm, summer's night with not a cloud in the sky?

During the drive back to Pete's house John experienced a growing feeling that he was slipping away from the real world into some alternative form of existence, as the reality of what he had done and what he was planning to do dawned on him. At first he was sure he was going to be caught, and made to answer for his crime – because that was what he had committed, a crime. At any moment, he knew, a pair, or pairs, of headlights would appear in front of, or behind, him, accompanied by blue flashing lights and sirens; he would be stopped, dragged out of the car, handcuffed and taken away to be punished. It did not happen. He carried on driving and was soon passing through the middle of South-newtown; in no time at all he was halfway between there and Asham, Bridges Junction a long way behind him, and he knew he had got away with it. Then the sense of detachment hit him, and it stayed with him throughout the rest of the journey back, and through the night, during which he found it difficult to sleep for more than a few hours, and through the long, long day that followed.

Later, when he looked back on that day, try as he might, he could not remember anything about it. He knew he was at Pete's house, he knew Pete was there too, but so focussed was he on what he was going to do that night that he had no memory of what they did, what they said, what they ate or drank – nothing.

Late that night John returned to the building site at Bridges Junction, again using Pete's car. He parked it in a different spot for fear of arousing suspicion. He left it unlocked again and, once more dressed like the Milk Tray man, headed towards the perimeter fence. Making sure that the security guard's van was not standing beside the main gates, he crossed over the road on the eastern side of the site and followed the fence up and around the southern end of it to a clump of bushes at its south-west corner, beside the narrow, concrete-surfaced access road that ran between the site fence and the high metal palings of the compound in which the railway control room and signal box stood. John crouched down in the bushes. Here he was shielded from sight, but had a clear view of the entrance. He pulled on the balaclava ski-mask and gloves, and settled down to wait.

Time passed, and events followed the pattern John had observed from the crane the night before. From time to time he glanced at the luminous dial of his watch, impatient to be on the move. From time to time he turned his head from the road and looked all around him, to make sure he was still concealed and, above all, that he was not being stalked by the dog – or by anything or anyone else.

At a little before two o'clock in the morning, the last few members of staff emerged from the building inside the compound, climbed into their cars and drove off into the night. The gate was held open again by the uniformed guard. As the last tail lights disappeared down the access road and turned out onto the main road at the bottom, the guard took one last look around, then pulled the gate shut and locked it with the padlock. As he walked away towards the back of the station John's heart rate increased; he had only about half an hour left to wait. That half-hour was the longest he had ever endured. During that time he experienced a range of emotions, from pessimism to euphoria. He wanted to get on with it; he wanted to run away and hide; he wanted to be sick; he wanted to pee; and then he wanted none of those things and was left just wondering what the hell he was doing there. At last, he saw the security guard ambling up the slope towards him, and he knew the waiting was over.

Make your stupid mind up, you idiot! he shouted silently to himself. Either do it or don't do it: do it or don't do it.

Make your mind up! Don't do it. Do it. Don't do it. DO IT!

The guard went into the compound, pushing the gate closed behind him. He slid the flat bolt noisily into place and hung the unlocked padlock back on it so that it looked as though it was closed, but in fact remained open. Then he walked across the compound and disappeared inside the building. That was John's cue to move. He took a deep breath, raised himself from the undergrowth and, in a crouching run, crossed the road to the fence and the gate. He reached up and took the padlock off, slid the bolt slowly back, hoping that it would not squeak. He was in luck, as neither the bolt nor the hinges made a sound as he entered. He stepped into the compound, pushing the gate closed and putting the bolt and padlock back in place behind him. It was a lax state of mind that led the guard not to lock up the compound when he was inside it. He assumed, John supposed, that his mere presence there was sufficient deterrent to anyone intent on entering the place. How wrong he was! John planned to stay there, locked in, to look around at his leisure after the guard had left, quitting the place through the unlocked gate when the man made his next visit. He positioned himself in the shadows behind a large van parked near the fence. Then the waiting began again.

The guard seemed to be inside the building for an eternity, but eventually he came out and, after his usual, cursory look around, made his way back to the gate in the fence and prepared to leave. He stepped out onto the road, shut and locked the gate, turned away and was gone. John did not move for another five minutes, long enough, he thought, for the guard to return to wherever it was he went to at the back of the station between his patrols of the compound. Then he moved to the front of the van and peered out cautiously. Seeing nobody, he left the shadows and walked across the compound to the side of the building, heading for the place where he had seen the guard enter, the night before.

The door was recessed in the wall and was deep in shadow. John hesitated slightly, feeling that the next step he would take, into the darkness, was truly a step into something new and unknown for him – a point of no return. Only then did it occur to him that he might not be able to take the step he considered so symbolic, because if the door was locked he was completely buggered. Tentatively, he reached out, grasped the knob and turned it; he pushed the door. It did not move. Cursing, he leant his weight against it. All of a sudden the door swung open, depositing him in an untidy heap on the floor inside.

Pulling himself to his feet and feeling rather stupid, John turned on his little torch to find out where he was. I'll bet the Milk Tray man never managed to pratfall through a doorway like that, he thought, otherwise he'd have squashed all his soft centres.

The beam of the torch revealed a corridor, with several doors on each side and a concrete staircase leading upwards at its far end. The doors were, he found, all locked and, as he had no tools for, or expertise in, picking locks, the staircase was his only option. He went up carefully and quietly. At the top, he found a short stretch of landing with another closed door at its far end. This swung open easily when he turned its knob and he found himself standing on the threshold of the control room: an open space where those he knew as signalmen worked. Now, with the inevitable introduction of computers to help them do the job, he had no idea what they should properly be called – Traffic Control and Direction Executives, or some such silly title, probably. He stepped in and looked around him. Against the walls in front of him and on his right, under the windows, were the consoles where the signalmen sat, looking out over the station and tracks. On his left, mounted high on the wall, was a huge diagram representing the area they controlled, with strips and pinpoints of light decorating its surface. These meant nothing to John. Also on his left, there was a line of three desks, of the kind usually found in offices where, he supposed, the supervisors or managers sat, with cupboards and bookshelves lined up behind them against the wall, under the diagram. In the centre of the room was a high table, topped with a glass-sided cover, under which he could see a large, open book.

A sudden realisation hit him, like a jolting shock: in planning this escapade he had spent all his time working out how he was going to get into the place, and none at all deciding what he was going to do when he got there. The truth of the matter was that, as with his opening of the spreadsheet, he had no clear idea what he was looking for, just the unshakeable belief that, whatever it was, he would recognise it when he found it. For the second time that proved to be exactly the case, as he walked slowly forward towards the book, lying under its glass cover. The light in the room was dim, but just bright enough for him to see that the pages of the book were made from a thick, heavy paper and that the writing on them had been done by hand, in ink, using an ornate, old-fashioned script. Across the width of the left-hand page lay a flat, thin piece of pale wood, not unlike a ruler, but with no markings on it, placed as if to underline the writing spread out across the page above it. He leant forward, to see more clearly what was written there.

'357 – Current isolation in the Bigton station sidings approaches,' he read aloud in a breathy whisper.

Looking up and down the pages, he could see that the other entries followed a similar pattern: first a number, apparently selected at random, placed on the far left-hand side of each page, then neat lines of text that, he realised as he read them, all appeared to be reasons why trains might be delayed or run late. This was, indeed, a discovery and a prize worth having. Leaving the book where it was for the time being, he took from one of the bookcases standing against the back wall of the room the largest and heaviest book he could find there. Returning to the table in the centre of the room, with this new book, he lifted the glass case off and set it down on the floor next to him. Then he took the Book of Reasons from the table-top, closed it, and tucked it under his arm, replacing it with the new book, which he let fall open somewhere near the middle before putting the glass cover back over it.

What now? he wondered, looking round. The desks, he decided. Look for anything you can find on the desks.

Moving back across the floor to stand in front of the first in the line of three, he shuffled quickly through the piles of paper and books lying on the desk-top, in the in- and out-trays there, but found nothing he thought would be of any use to him. So he moved sideways, to the second in the line. The first document he picked up was a folder, holding a large number of sheets of paper that all, at first glance, appeared to be similar, if not identical, but which on closer examination proved to be completed forms of some kind, the basic format of which was indeed identical, but with details entered on them that were different in each case. After looking at a number of these, John flipped the cover of the folder shut and read its front label: 'Schedule of Engi-neering Works – BJ Control Sectors – Southern Region – Current Year'. The Perma-way logo was printed neatly underneath. Then, for no real reason at all, John looked up into the corner of the room on his left-hand side, where the walls and ceiling met – straight into the lens of a closed-circuit television camera.

The guard returned to his lair, on the island that formed platforms three and four of the station, after his patrol, looking forward to a mug of tea and reading his paper.

He made his way into his control room, sat down and raised the mug to his mouth. As he did so, he caught sight in the corner of his eye of a movement on one of the CCTV screens. He turned, then sat forward with a jerk, spilling his tea. The screen showed the inside of the signal box and a figure clad entirely in black, a mask covering his face, except for his eyes which stared into the camera. The guard saw his job, his salary, his mortgage, his pension and his future slipping away from him, unless he acted swiftly. He slammed his mug down, grabbed his heavy torch, which would also serve as a handy club if necessary, and set off at a run.

John swore loudly.

Get out of here, now, he told himself.

But I haven't done what I came here to do.

I've got the book. That's got to be worth something. Get out.

That might not be enough. If it isn't, all this has been a waste of time. I'll be no further forward, and I won't be able to come back, that's for sure.

If you stay there's a real risk you won't be going anywhere. The guard could be here any second, and if you get caught . . . MOVE!

He thrust the folder between the pages of the book and snapped it shut. Then he ran.

The guard puffed his way up the road to the compound. The intruder had obviously slipped in through the unlocked gate while he was on his last patrol, so there would be no damage to the fences, no forced entry. The first thing he had to do was get the bloody man out of there. After that he must find out whether there was any damage or if anything had been taken. If there was, he would have to fake a forced entry to cover his incompetence, then raise the alarm. If not, he was in the clear. There were no video recorders attached to the CCTV system, so he was the only one who would ever see the pictures the camera in the control room had captured; they were a thing of the moment and were now gone forever. If there was no visible damage and nothing had been taken, he was all right; his career, his pension and his future were safe.

John went back down the stairs as quickly as he could, and moved swiftly along the corridor to the outside door, where he paused. He pulled it open a crack and peered through the gap, expecting that at any second it would be torn out of his hand and the guard would be there in front of him. Outside it was quiet and deserted. He moved forward, pausing again in the inky blackness of the recess and looking warily around. The compound and the road alongside it were still deserted.

He left the safety of the shadows and ran across to the van he had sheltered behind before, stopping in the darkness behind it while he rehearsed in his mind what the next step had to be, and waited for the guard to arrive.

The guard was a big man with plenty of muscle, but he was not particularly fit. He knew he should exercise more, but he was too lazy, and after running up the road to the compound he was short of breath. He stopped at the corner of the fence, breathing heavily, and peered in. Seeing nothing, he moved slowly along the fence to the gate, taking out the bunch of keys he kept on a chain in his trouser pocket, and selecting the one he needed.

John heard him coming and made ready.

The guard opened the gate and stepped warily into the compound, his torch held out in front of him like the weapon he intended it to be.

Peering around the corner of the van, John knew that this was the time; it had to be now, before the guard had time to shut the gate and lock them both in again. Leaving the cover of the shadows, he ran between the van and the fence and launched himself at the man.

The guard sensed, more than heard, him coming, and looked up as the book hit him full in the face. He went down like the proverbial sack of potatoes, stunned rather than knocked out, but it was enough. John leapt through the open gate, tucked the book back under his arm and ran for all he was worth to where he had left Pete's car. The guard was down for several minutes while his head spun and throbbed. Eventually he managed to sit up and, after a few minutes more, his head cleared enough for him to be able to look around and make sense of what he saw. The gate stood wide open again and there was no sign of the intruder. He hoped, he prayed, that he had gone, slipped away into the night, never to return. Carefully, he stood up, not wanting to move too fast, and held onto the side of the gate until his head stopped spinning. Not wanting to make the same mistake twice on the same day, he pushed it shut and locked it, then made his way to the control room building. The doors leading off the ground-floor corridor were still shut and locked. Upstairs, the control room itself was peaceful. He looked round quickly from the doorway. The control consoles were undamaged; the small table still stood in the centre of the room with its book and glass case resting on top of it; the desks were tidy and apparently undisturbed. His spirits rose as his worst fears evaporated. The intruder had gone; nothing had been damaged or obviously disturbed; he was safe. There was no need to call the police, to fake a forced entry in order to hide his incompetence. He went back down the stairs and, after one final turn around the compound, he locked up and returned to his lair in the station.

Best to let sleeping dogs lie he told himself.

So he did.

8

Week Three: Day One – On the Monday

The sun did not rise clear and shining into a bright blue sky on that Monday morning. Instead, it was hidden behind a veil of low cloud and mist that swirled around the windows and clung to the walls of the Bridges Junction control room, a persistent light drizzle that damped the glass and made the world outside look even more bleak and obscure. It was cold.

Footsteps echoed on the stairs as the early morning procession ascended to the control room from the floor below, then gathered around the table in the centre of the room, with its precious book under its glass case. The most junior person present executed the customary routine: he raised the glass case, lifted the book, shut the book, offered it to the person who had the honour of deciding where it should be opened that day, and waited while thumbs were inserted with eyes closed. He let the book fall open on his outstretched palms at the chosen place, then looked down – at a double-page colour photograph of the Flying Scotsman in full steam.

'What the fuck . . . ?'

He found himself holding a copy of a heavy book entitled *Great Railway Journeys of the World*.

John slept long and late that morning after his excursion to Bridges Junction station. When he did, finally, wake up it was broad daylight outside his bedroom window and what had happened the night before felt remote to him, like events in a barely-remembered dream. But it hadn't been a dream. It was all real, and the book he had stolen, which was lying at the top of his bed, half-buried under the pillow, bore witness to the truth of what he had done. He remembered the drive home: the fear, the recklessness, driving as fast as he dared, certain that this time there would be lights, there would be sirens, there would be pursuit, arrest, trial, imprisonment.

After a while he had calmed down and taken stock of where he was: miles away from Asham in the wrong direction, to the east of Southnewtown. There was plenty of petrol in the tank, so he decided to take a circuitous route back to Pete's house, by turning south on the first major road he encountered and following it until he came to the coast, then turning west until he reached the outskirts of Bigton. From there he knew he could head north and westwards, along a series of country roads that would bring him back to Asham without going anywhere near either Bridges Junction or Southnewtown, two places he was very keen to avoid just then.

When he got himself out of bed and went downstairs, Pete was not there, having left earlier in the day to 'fix' another of his clients' computers. He had left a note for John in the kitchen.

'Had a look at your spreadsheet, mate – hope you don't mind – remind me to teach you how to cover your tracks on the computer sometime. I don't know what it's used for, but I'd say it's all set up for computerisation, so the data in it can be input and used as the basis for something else – something that combines its info. with other stuff, to carry out some function or the other. I know that all sounds a bit vague and I haven't explained it very well. We can talk about it when I get back, if you want. See you later, Pete.'

John did not see Pete again, as his friend had not returned

when John came to leave. This was often the way with Pete's work; it was difficult to predict how long some of it might take, as it was often not clear exactly what his clients wanted from him until he arrived at their premises. Once started he liked to carry on, undisturbed, until he had finished and was confident that what he had done was working properly. John was envious of his friend in some ways. To be so interested, so absorbed, so rewarded, by the job that you did was an experience with which John was completely unfamiliar. Roland Smythe had made sure of that, and the corporate stupidity that was PLGC's HR department did nothing to help. But John also had to acknowledge that Pete's lack of routine would not have suited him: the long and odd hours, the missed meals, the missed sleep, the uncertainty about where the next day's work might come from – none of that was for him.

These thoughts continued to occupy him as he left Pete's house, not long before midnight, to walk to his own. It was risky, he knew, but he had decided it was a risk he must take, because there were things he needed: not least some clean clothes.

As he walked through the darkened streets he wondered if his house was being watched and, if it was, how he was going to get in and, more importantly, back out again, unseen. Dressed in black but without the ski-mask, he melted into the darkness of the alley behind his house. It was deserted as far as he could see. He walked slowly until he reached his back gate. With a last, fearful glance around him, he opened it and went in.

Inside the house the air smelt stale and musty, even after only a few days of being closed up. He shut the back door behind him and locked it, leaving the key on the inside, in case he needed to leave in a hurry. He walked through the kitchen and dining room, heading for the foot of the stairs in the dark, not wanting to give his presence away by turning on any of the lights, trying all the while to stay quiet, to listen for any hint of a sound that would tell him he was not alone. There was nothing.

Upstairs in his bedroom he drew the curtains across the window, but still he did not turn on the light, preferring to use the pencil-thin beam of his torch to light his way. He reached into his wardrobe and pulled out a brown leather suitcase. Opening drawers and cupboards, he half-filled the suitcase with clothes, then went to the bathroom for his washing and shaving kit. From secret places he took money, bank cards and his passport. He went back downstairs to find his mobile phone, which he thought he might have left on the arm of his chair, but he could not find it, even with the glow of the streetlights shining through the open curtains. As he was about to leave the room the house phone rang. Without thinking he picked up the receiver and held it against his ear.

'Hello,' he said, warily.

As soon as the person on the other end of the line spoke, John recognised his voice: it was Wright Arse.

'You have something that belongs to us, Mr Biddle.'

'Who is this?'

'I think you already know the answer to that question, John.'

'What do you mean by 'us', Adrian? Are you now a Perma-way employee, or still just their paid lackey?'

'Dealing with me, dealing with them – it's all one and the same thing,' Wright replied with icy calm. 'Your answer tells me you know what I'm talking about, John; you do have what we want.'

'I don't remember saying that.'

'But you don't deny it.'

Silence.

'Are you prepared to return it?'

'How can I return something I never had in the first place? What is it you're looking for, anyway?'

'I'd advise you to be careful, John. You don't know what you're dealing with here. We want our property back, and we want it back now. If we don't get it. . . well, I'll leave that to your imagination. Do you understand what I'm telling you here?'

'No, actually I don't,' John said defiantly. 'I'm feeling a little slow tonight. It must be the lateness of the hour. You'll have to be more specific I'm afraid.'

'The railway can be a dangerous place, John – all those speeding trains, platform edges, dark tunnels, high bridges, faulty carriage door locks, live rails. Have you ever seen a body that's been hit by a speeding train, John? It's not a pretty sight, I can tell you. Very nasty. Very unpleasant. Am I making myself clear enough now?'

'Are you threatening me?'

'We want our property back, and we always get what we want. . . eventually. . . one way or the other. It would be a shame to think you were going to have to spend what's left of your life constantly looking over your shoulder.'

'I don't have it,' John said, not untruthfully because it was not actually with him in the house just then; it was still at Pete's place.

'Don't let us down, John – just don't. Take this as your one and only warning.'

'Take what?'

The line went dead. Seconds later the window of the sitting room burst in with a crash. John jumped back in alarm, and his heart stopped momentarily as he saw the object that had rolled across the floor and come to rest against the toe of his shoe. It was a petrol-bomb, a Molotov cocktail, a glass bottle filled with a colourless liquid, a burning rag projecting from its neck. Rooted to the spot, blessing his luck that it had not broken as it crashed through the window, he yet remained indecisive to the point of inaction. His mind raced. He could try to extinguish it. He could pick it up and throw it back out through the broken window into the front garden or the street beyond, or out through the back door into the garden on that side of the house. But if it went wrong, whatever he did, he could be hurt, or worse, killed.

His dilemma was resolved by events. The flaming rag spluttered and went out, extinguished by what turned out to be water inside the bottle. This was no attempt on his life. It was only a warning of what could happen if he did not return the book – or, he realised later, what might happen to him after he had returned it. Suddenly, he was angry. His heart pounded as the adrenalin began to surge through his body. He ran to the front door, threw it open and charged out into the street. It was quiet, as it always was at that time of the night. The streetlights were bright and harsh. The only sound was the engine of a distant car, its tail lights just visible as it braked sharply and hurtled round the corner at the end of the road, several hundred yards away.

John ran back into the house. He knew he had to leave, and could not return until all of this was over. The house would just have to look after itself. He slammed the front door and ran up the stairs, where the suitcase he had packed lay open on the bed. Everything he thought he would need was inside it, so he threw the lid shut, picked it up and went back down the stairs. He moved quietly in case Wright Arse or any of his men had come back after the episode with the bottle. As far as he could make out, there was no-one there, so he went into the hall, and from there into the dining room. It was dark as there were no street lights outside its window and the curtains were still closed, but he had lived there for so long without changing anything that he did not need light to find his way around. He opened the drawer of the sideboard where he kept the exercise books he used as his train diaries. He took them all out and put them in the suitcase, on top of his clothes. Then he let himself out of the back door and locked it after him.

In the garden it was almost as dark as it had been inside the house. Thick cloud hid the moon and stars. That was all to the good, John thought. Carrying the suitcase in one hand, the other held out in front of him, he made his way along the fence that divided his garden from that of his neighbour, until he found the gap that he had used the first time he had sought to avoid Adrian Wright's Arse men. He followed the same route, though it was infinitely more difficult in the dark than it had been in daylight, and discovery far more likely than it had been on the former occasion.

Carefully he made his way behind the row of houses, crossing the heads of their gardens and squeezing through gaps in their fences. Remembering how he had done it before, he counted the gardens he crossed, so he would know when he should turn and walk down the path to an unlocked gate leading into the alley. He carried on walking. He carried on counting and, at the appointed place, turned, walked down to the gate, opened it and slipped quietly into the alley.

Out there it was also quiet and dark, but there was a difference: the far ends of the alley were lit up by the lights on the streets that ran across them at right angles. John paused with his back pressed firmly against the fence of the garden behind him, trying to make sure that any silhouette he made with his body against the light at either end of that dark corridor was as small as it could possibly be. He stood there like that for several long minutes, breathing deeply, turning his head first one way and then the other, looking for anyone who might be waiting for him in the darkness. He did not see anyone, but that did not mean they were not there; they could easily be standing with their backs pressed up against the fences or walls just as he was, or in the recesses he knew were formed by several of the gates along the row. What should he do now? If they were there, he could not simply walk out of the alley, either one way or the other, because they would catch him. But what was the alternative? His mind raced through the choices, limited though they were. And as he thought, a plan emerged, involving the houses in the row opposite him, and a gate that he could just about see in the fence on that far side. It was a short way up from where he stood, just visible in the faint light spilling into the darkness from the street at the far end. It was a risk, but one he had to take. It was his only chance.

John took a deep breath and made ready. He counted himself down, to make sure he did not change his mind.

'Three, two, one – GO!'

He ran diagonally across the alley, grabbing the latch on the gate on the far side, praying that it was not locked. It opened and he threw himself through it onto the ground in the garden beyond. He reached out a leg and pushed it shut. From somewhere in the distance he heard a voice shouting, then the sound of running feet. He pulled himself to his knees and turned to the gate he had just burst through, frantically searching for the bolt he hoped would be there. His fingers closed on it and slid it home. Clambering to his feet, he grasped the suitcase and began picking his way up the garden towards the house. He knew it would not be easy for his pursuers to find out which garden he had gone into, not now that the gate behind him was locked. He also knew that the houses on this side of the alley were different from his; they were semi-detached, and had gaps between them, gaps that should offer him a route through to the street on the further side. What he did not know was whether the pathway from this back garden through to its front was blocked by a side-extension or other obstruction he could not yet see, or whether he might fall into a pond or hole in the dark before he ever got that far. His progress along the length of the garden was slow at first, but accelerated when he heard the click of a gate latch, quite clearly in the still of the night.

Suddenly the air was full of bright white light, blinding after the darkness. Because recent events had placed him firmly at the centre of his own universe, where everything that happened related only to him and what he was doing, John thought that he had been discovered and that those who were chasing him were responsible for the light. But then he realised that could not be the case as it was not coming from behind him but from in front. Its source was high on the back wall of the next house in the row; high enough for its over-sensitive infra-red detector to have picked up his presence and turned it on, bathing both gardens in radiance, except for a narrow strip along the side of the high wooden fence dividing the two. This remained in shadow. Realising he was in full view of anyone who might happen to look out of a window in the back of the house, or the upstairs windows of the houses on either side – or, more importantly, anyone looking over the fence at the bottom of the garden, John skipped sideways into the shadow and quickened his pace.

The dog that lived in the house next door was mean, but by no means dumb. He knew that if he roamed about the garden at night, which he was free to do, he would turn on the light on the back of his master's house and the darkness he valued so much would be lost. So, not unhappily, he kept to his kennel where it was warm, dry, comfortable and, best of all, dark. When, however, the light came on he was always ready to venture outside to discover the reason why. When he did, he was invariably grumpy and spoiling for a fight.

John heard the soft growling and the padding of heavy feet on the far side of the fence and knew the fence was the only thing standing between him and another encounter with a ferocious canine. He walked on even faster, painfully aware that there might be holes in the fence which he did not know about, or that the dog, if it was a big one, might be able to jump over it. From the far end of the garden both he and the dog heard a sharp click as a hand fell on a gate latch. This was followed by the sound of someone scrabbling up the outside of a wooden fence – a fence housing a gate which had been found to be locked. The dog left off stalking John and bounded down the garden in the direction from which the noises had come. John reached the back wall of the house, hoping that whoever it was in the alley had been fooled into thinking that he had gone into the garden of the house with the security light and was about to get a nasty surprise. As he crossed the back of the house and turned down the side of it, the volley of barking and the sudden, long scream that shattered the peace of the night led him to believe his hopes had been fulfilled.

John did not wait to find out, however, but hurried down the side of the house with renewed anxiety as to whether his pathway to the road, and freedom, was clear. The omens were not good, because where he had hoped he would see the orange glow of the street lights in the gap between the gable ends of the houses, he could see only darkness. Advancing more slowly now, he groped his way in through the open back of what he realised must be some kind of lean-to, past parked bikes and shelves of gardening equipment, to a door at the front. He ran his hands down one side of it and found only hinges. He ran them down the other and found a lock, with a round, plastic knob, and a key. He turned it and the lock made a reassuring click. He twisted the knob and – joy! – the door swung open, letting the light from the street lamps spill in across the floor. He slipped through into the front garden of the house, transferring the key from the inside to the outside of the door, pulling it shut and locking it behind him, in case one of the Arses managed to guess what had happened and where he had gone. Then he dropped the key into his pocket and took it with him.

The street – that part of it he could see – was deserted. Looking from side to side, he satisfied himself that the rest of it was in the same state, then set out at a brisk walk, prepared to run if necessary, towards the station.

As he walked, he kept a good lookout around him, to make sure that he was not being pursued or followed – and which of those two words was the more accurate? Pursued or followed? If it was him they wanted, they could simply have burst into his house while he was there and grabbed him, instead of going through the elaborate farce with the fake petrol bomb. If they thought the book was at his house with him, they could have collected it when they collected him, and they would then have had everything they wanted. No, what was happening suggested that they knew the book was not at the house, either because they had already searched it, or because they knew he had not been there since the book had been taken. It was clear from the timing of the phone call and the trick with the petrol bomb that they had known when he had arrived, so the house was being watched, *and* they were sure that he did not have the book with him when he arrived. The odds were, therefore, against their trying to capture him; they would follow him in the hope that he would lead them to where the book was hidden. Either way, he needed to shake them off; as soon as they had the book he became expendable.

On his way to the station he worked out a plan, in case another Arse man picked up his scent, which was quite likely because he had no choice but to rejoin the road he lived in just before the station approach peeled off it and, for a short while at least, he would be in full view of anyone who might be lurking around outside his house. His fears were justified. When he turned the last corner into the road he lived in, he glanced to his right, towards the front of his house, and saw a man in the distance, looking his way and talking into his sleeve, the way he had seen American Secret Service agents doing in some of the spy films he watched. He was, John thought, either an Arse man or a madman. The man saw him and started running his way: he was an Arse man. John fled, but was hampered by his age and his suitcase. However, he had a head start and made it to the back entrance of the station with more than enough time for what he was planning to do.

The ticket barriers were closed against him when he got there, but that was to his advantage. He had his season ticket clutched in his hand, and he was certain his pursuer would not have one too. He ran up the short flight of steps to the barriers, panting hard, and thrust his ticket into the machine. The barriers swung open. He ran between them, taking his ticket out as he went, and heard the reassuring sound of their closing behind him. He ran on up the concrete steps to the footbridge above. Halfway across he heard the man chasing him arrive at the barriers, and his first, brutish attempt to plough through them – a crash and a grunt of pain. By then John was most of the way across the bridge, and could not see his pursuer take a step back, leap athletically onto the console dividing the aisles which the barriers blocked, and jump down lightly on the other side ready to continue his pursuit up the stairs. John turned the corner at the far end of the footbridge and headed down towards the station foyer and its main entrance.

At the foot of that staircase the second set of ticket barriers was closed, and manned that night by a burly, irritable 'Revenue Enforcement Officer' (ticket inspector) by the name of Ken Pratt. This individual was in a particularly bad mood that night because it was his birthday and, instead of enjoying a boozy night with his wife and friends in his local pub, followed by an Indian meal, as he had planned, he had been made to cover for a co-worker who had called in at the last minute, allegedly sick, and who was, in all probability, in a pub somewhere else, toasting Ken's health and laughing his head off. To make matters worse, he suspected that his so-called 'best mate' would be taking advantage of his absence to make a move on his wife, whose loyalty and fidelity he had had reason to doubt for some time. In fact, Ken Pratt was spoiling for a fight.

John arrived at the foot of the stairs first, breathless, panting, and exhausted, unused to all this exercise. Seeing him descend apparently in some distress and struggling with a suitcase, Ken opened the large single barrier for him and nodded him through with a cursory glance at his ticket. The next man down was also in a hurry, but was in good physical shape, more used to rushing about, and, Ken thought, probably someone who worked out to stay fit – but he had no ticket and did not seem to understand when Ken told him he must show a valid ticket or pay a penalty. He also did not understand that it might not be such a good idea to try to push his way past someone of Ken's size. He took Ken by surprise with a shoulder charge to the chest; Ken went over backwards, bouncing off the ticket machine behind him and falling forwards again as his attacker brushed past. With a bellow of rage, the inspector reached out as he fell, clamped both hands firmly around a skinny ankle, and pulled.

John looked back as he heard Ken's shout, just in time to see the other man hit the floor face first. Ken slid forward and knelt on his assailant's back, fists swinging, overwhelmed by anger and frustration. Ken bellowed, the other screamed, and John slipped out through the doors of the main entrance and headed for the taxi-rank, knowing that his adversary was likely to be kept busy for some time, first by the ticket inspector, and then by the accident and emergency department of the local hospital.

Two down. How many more to go? John thought, and carried on running.

The night-time taxi drivers in Asham were a breed apart

from the gentlemen who did the job during the hours of daylight – they had to be, to hold their own against some of the types they encountered in the small hours. John walked swiftly across the station forecourt towards the taxi-rank where the drivers stood in a group talking. He picked out the most disreputable-looking of them, the one most likely to accept his challenge.

'Are you free?' John asked.

'I sure am, guv'. This one's mine,' he said, motioning towards a nondescript Vauxhall.

John got in.

'Where we goin' then?' the driver asked, looking over his shoulder.

'I need to get to Crowcopse golf course, and can you make sure we're not followed?'

'I sure can, mate,' the driver responded gamely.

He started the engine and the car rocketed away from the taxi-rank with a screech of tyres. He steered straight ahead for a short distance as they picked up speed, then swung the wheel hard over to the right, shooting through one lane of traffic and joining the other in a gap that was not really there, accompanied by a forest of brake lights and a cacophony of blaring horns.

And try not to attract any attention while you're doing it, John thought, then slid across from one side of the seat to the other as the driver swung the wheel hard over to the left, entering and leaving a roundabout without reducing speed then accelerated away.

The buildings on either side of them became a blur as they raced past: the post office, the magistrate's court, the fire station, police station, sixth-form college and hospital. At the end of the road they jumped the red traffic lights and made a screeching right turn on what felt to John, now thrown against the window on the left, like only two of the four available wheels. The driver straightened the car up, shot it through another set of lights just as they changed to red, then stamped hard on the brakes and turned violently to the left, almost mounting the kerb as he swung round the corner, and nearly ploughing into the back of the first in a line of parked cars on the right-hand side of the road. Again he accelerated as he straightened up, then glanced in the mirror at the empty road behind them and John's ashen face.

'What a rush, eh?' he said. John had no words and no breath with which to reply. 'Nothing behind us now,' the driver told him, and John looked round to confirm his statement.

'In that case, I have a change of destination to announce.' Giving Pete's address he said, 'I want to stop there to collect something. Then I want to go to The Boltons – to a cheap, but clean, hotel somewhere near the station. Is that OK?'

'If you can pay, then it's OK,' the driver said, with laconic rhyme. 'All right if I slow down a bit now? I don't like to drive too fast; it's not safe. Can you remind me of that address you just gave me?'

Not safe! Tell me about it, thought John, rubbing gingerly at the side of his face, bruised from its encounters with the cab windows.

Although there was no appreciable reduction in either the speed or recklessness of the driver, they arrived at Pete's house safe, sound and unaccompanied. The driver waited outside with the engine running while John went inside. The house was in darkness; Pete was either still out somewhere or fast asleep in bed. John collected the book and the printout of the spreadsheet. He left Pete a note saying he had gone to ground and thanking him for everything. Then he went returned to the taxi.

Their trip to The Boltons was uneventful: no pursuing cars, no scares, no panics – and not long after leaving Asham

John found himself settling down for the night behind the locked door of a room in the Tour-Inn, a chain hotel on the main road not far from the station and the Army Surplus Store. The taxi driver had grinned broadly when John paid him and added a generous tip for his trouble.

'I'd have done the same for nothing, mate – for the sheer hell of it,' he said.

'Would it be possible for you to keep this trip a secret? Not mention it,' John asked, 'if anyone comes trying to find out where you dropped me?'

'Oh, I wouldn't worry about that,' the driver told him. 'They'll have to find me first. I don't come from round here. I'm not really a taxi driver at all. I'd only stopped to ask directions when you grabbed me, and I thought, Why look a gift horse. . . and all that?

Then he got back into his car and screeched off into the night, leaving John wondering if the early part of their journey would have been any different if he had not told him he did not want to be followed.

He turned off the light, stretched out in the unfamiliar bed in the darkness of the unfamiliar room, and fell asleep almost immediately.

9

Week Three: Day Two – On the Tuesday

In the morning the skies had cleared and the sunshine was back again. For the second consecutive day the trains ran almost faultlessly, delivering grateful workers to their destinations on time, and leaving them hoping they would be just as grateful at the end of the day, when they were on their way home.

John woke up late, wondering where he was for a moment or two, before his brain woke itself up too and his memory began to function properly. When he was dressed, shaved and ready to face the day, he went down for breakfast, taking with him the book, the folder of papers belonging to Perma-way, the printout of the spreadsheet and his railway diaries, all locked in the suitcase, which he stood on the floor beside the table while he ate. He knew it looked odd, but he did not care; he would not have felt comfortable leaving them in the room while he was absent. Besides, if he was discovered and had to make a quick exit, he needed to have them with him.

His appetite satisfied, he returned to his room, but not before he had been to a convenience store a short way along the road, to buy some things; sellotape, a pair of scissors, a newspaper, some sandwiches for his lunch and a cheap transistor radio. When he got back he hung the 'Do not disturb' notice on the outside of his door, locked himself in the room and settled down to study and to think.

The first part of his day's work saw him sitting on the bed flicking through the pages of the newspaper, looking for any reference it might contain to the theft he had carried out two nights before, while listening to a local radio station for similar news.

Of John's exploits there was no mention in the paper, nor on the radio. He had not really thought that there would be. Perma-way would hardly be likely to tell the police, 'The book we use to delay the trains has been stolen, and we'd like you to help us get it back.' (At least that was what John had convinced himself was its purpose.) No, the job of finding it had been entrusted to the agents of Arse. He had to find out their secret before they found him.

He shut the paper, turned off the radio, moved across to the desk and sat down, with the stolen book resting on it in front of him. The cover announced its title in gold letters:

London, Bigton & Southern Coastal
Railway Company
A Record of Reasons for Disturbance
to the Progress of Trains

It was a formal and rather flowery way of saying: 'Why the trains run late.' He opened the cover and began reading. Each page had on it a number of these reasons, neatly hand-written in black ink, by someone with an excellent and beautiful hand. The early entries were numbered in ascending order, starting at '1'. As he flicked through the pages, John saw that these earliest entries related to the breakdown of steam-driven locomotives, and all had been neatly crossed through, as they were not relevant to an age of electric- and diesel-powered trains. Further on he began to find reasons such as broken rails, frozen points, and other track-related problems; then excuses to do with electricity and, finally, a new group relating computer errors of one sort another. These later entries had been made randomly, dotted about here and there on the pages of the book, although the numbering appeared sequential – it was in chronological order. Altogether there were thousands of them, each one different from those preceding or following it. Before he had started reading The Book he had not imagined there could be so many ways trains could be delayed.

Does life imitate The Book, or does The Book imitate life? he wondered. In the case of the trains, he felt pretty sure it had begun as the latter and developed into the former. At some time or another, the work that had commenced as a labour of love for someone who obviously cherished the task, had been hi-jacked, perverted from its original aim of creating a record of past events, to become the predictor of events yet to occur.

He looked again at the numbers running down the sides of the pages, flicking through them, searching for the earliest of the entries not crossed out. He found them and studied their numbers and the numbers of those that followed. They prompted a memory of some of the figures he had seen on the Perma-way web site. He decided to assemble the jigsaw of the spreadsheet.

He lifted the thick pile of paper out of the suitcase, placed it carefully on the edge of the duvet and started to tape the pages to the wall, one by one, assembling the spreadsheet so he could see, if not all of it, at least a large part. He decided to concentrate or the most recent part of the spreadsheet, the part that would match most closely with what he could remember had been happening lately on the part of the network with which he was familiar. A large part of the wall was quickly covered in pieces of paper attached by sticky tape.

He then collected 'The Book of Excuses' from the desk and his diaries from the suitcase and sat down on the edge of the bed facing the paper-covered wall, The Book on one side of him and the diaries on the other. Reading from the bottom upwards, he went slowly through the spreadsheet, looking for entries he thought might involve delays to the trains on the Asham line. As he found them, he entered their details in an unused exercise book he found on the bottom of the pile.

When he had a fair quantity of data written down, he turned to The Book of Excuses and looked up each entry, using the number employed to identify it on the spreadsheet, to find out what The Book gave as the reason for the delay. Then he looked for the same incident in his diaries to see what he had recorded for that day. Time after time the reason given in The Book turned out to be more or less what he had recorded in his diary, from the information provided on the trains or at stations. The evidence was clear: those running the railway were deliberately delaying the trains in order to gain extra income. Two things, however, remained obscure: first, where was the money coming from – apart from the mysterious reference to 'RPI' in the spreadsheet? Second, and more important, how had he become involved so deeply in all of this in the first place? What clue was he still missing? What else did he have to look at that might help him?

Remembering the folder of papers he had taken from the Bridges Junction control room, he retrieved it from the suitcase and laid it on the desk. He made himself a cup of tea – always a good thing to have by your side when there is some serious thinking to be done – pulled up the chair, opened the folder and started to read. For the next two hours, he read sheet after sheet recording details of repairs to broken rails, defective signals, failed power supplies, subsiding or rotting sleepers, missing rail clips and a host of other problems that had needed to be sorted out.

Why on earth do they need to invent reasons to delay the trains, when they've already got this lot to do it for them?

he thought. It can only be an indication of how greedy they've become as the years have passed.

By now he was beginning to get tired, and more than a little jaded. He began to think he would never find what he was looking for, so that when finally he did stumble across it he almost overlooked its significance. It began with what must have been a larger project than most, composed of a series of small pieces of work: installing new cables alongside specific lengths of track, constructing concrete bases for various items of plant and equipment, then installing those items – power supply cabinets, communications connections cabinets, masts, aerials, booster stations, etc. Finally, trackside access was to be arranged for RP engineers to test and commission the system. John examined several further sheets before he realised with a start what he had just read: '. . .trackside access for RP engineers.' He went back and found the reference then went back further and read through the whole section again more carefully. He was reading about a project to improve mobile phone reception for train users; references to 'the network' could apply equally to the mobile phone system and to the railway itself.

John's mind filled with memories of people sitting on trains that were slowing down, stopping and stopped: old men, young men, old women, young women, children, all pulling out mobile phones, dialling and announcing, 'It's me. I'm on a train!' He had found it, and, he had to admit, it was brilliant. 'RP' was Roamer-Phone and RPI was 'Roamer-Phone Income'. The railway companies delayed the trains, the passengers used their mobiles to tell everyone they knew about it, Roamer-Phone's income went up and they paid the rail companies a slice of the proceeds. All those companies had to do was make sure the money they were given exceeded the fines they had to pay for late-running and they were in profit – making money for free. That was what the spreadsheet was telling him.

But where and how do I come into it all? he asked himself.

He lay on the bed and stared at the ceiling. He had some more thinking to do – but where was he to start? Then he remembered Pete's note, telling him he thought the spreadsheet had been put together as a means of allowing the data it contained to be input to some kind of computer programme, where it would be combined with other data.

Why? What other data? The data I produced? Could those two sets of data be combined, and if so, what would be the benefit?'

At this point John made an intellectual leap and jumped to a conclusion he knew, instantly and instinctively, must be right. It offered an explanation for everything that had happened – nothing else did.

The two sets of data were, he decided, intended to be combined in a computer programme that would take over the function of 'The Book of Excuses' and determine the reasons used to delay trains in the future and generate income from Roamer-Phone. The function of the programme would be to generate those excuses in such a way that the Roamer-Phone income would be maximised and the fines levied by OFFTOSS would be minimised, using the best and most productive excuses as often as possible, while at the same time not using them so often that they no longer appeared to be random. The spreadsheet information provided the data on the best excuses for delays. The information he had given Perma-way would be used to regulate how often each of the excuses could be used without attracting suspicion – by having too many suicides in too short a space of time, or too many sick passengers on trains, for example.

With that realisation, everything that had happened, and was still happening to him, made sense. The Book was 'reason': it was full of reasons. The computer programme was also 'reason', but it was a step further on: a development which made it 'beyond reason'. Perma-way already had the spreadsheet. He had turned out to be the person who could provide them with the rest of the data they needed, so he became their 'man beyond reason'. But he was not supposed to know any of that, so when Martin Adams had blurted it out without thinking, John had become a potential security risk and the chain of events that had led him to where he now was had been set in motion. What they were doing was a revelation. It was brilliant. It was also highly illegal, and they deserved to be exposed and punished for it. Unless, of course, he could find something better to do with his knowledge. In that moment, his transformation was completed. The old John Biddle was now a thing of the past; a new one had taken its place, prepared to do things its predecessor would never even have dreamed of doing. Now John did have a dream, and the more he thought about it, the more he believed that its realisation was possible, and within his reach.

He stayed where he was for a long time, staring unseeingly upwards and thinking. For almost the first time in his life he was being presented with an opportunity, a chance to do something for himself – and he was about to take it without being told to, or that he could or should, by somebody else. Its achievement would require considerable thought and a definite plan but that could all be worked out later.

Since possession of The Book on its own was worth enough for Adrian Wright to threaten to kill him, it was highly likely that all the evidence he had in his possession – The Book, the spreadsheet, the folder of work orders and his diaries – was something he could persuade Perma-way to part with money to get their hands on, provided he was clever enough. If he was really clever, he might persuade them to part with a considerable amount of money.

As he lay there he was torn by powerful and conflicting emotions. On the one hand, if he could pull this off, he would be hugely rich, and could say goodbye to PLGC and, particularly, Roland Smythe. On the other hand the thought of leaving behind everything that was solid and familiar, was enormously unsettling, particularly for someone whose very existence had been built on a bedrock of steadiness, solidity and routine. What he now proposed to do threw all of that away – in favour of what? A future that was uncertain. His excitement was tempered by something that felt like fear but was not. If he had been forced to name it he might have called it homesickness – a longing to retain the warmth and security of the familiar.

Then a pungent memory asserted itself – the memory of a night not long before all this had started. He had been out to the pub behind the station with his friends. On the way back, on his own in the darkness, a train had arrived at the station, and he remembered having felt suddenly envious of the people getting off – those who would be expected home shortly, by someone who was waiting for them – and he contrasted that with his arrival to a dark and empty house. And in that moment he knew that homesickness was not about missing a place, and he knew that to make this work he could not do it alone; he had to have someone to go with him, and that someone was Angela.

He sat up quickly, suddenly invigorated, suddenly hungry, suddenly filled with a new determination and purpose – that he knew what he wanted. Now he had to work out how he could get it. As he ate his sandwiches he began to formulate a plan. It began with the idea of escape; quickly and to a far-away place where he – no, the two them, he and Angela – would be difficult to trace. But where? South America: a distant, mysterious and romantic place, favourite for centuries past with renegades fleeing from Europe. Escaped convicts, political exiles, war criminals, all had gone there and been able to disappear. And it was not expensive to live well there; a million pounds could go a long way and last a very long time. But where in that vast continent should he choose? He knew almost nothing about the place beyond the names of a few of its cities and a few of its countries: Rio de Janeiro, Sao Paulo, Brasilia; Argentina, Peru, Brazil. Then he remembered the recent announcement of the start of scheduled flights by Novice Airlines, owned and run by the people's favourite entrepreneur, Dick Stonnick, between High Weald Airport and Caracas, which he knew was somewhere in South America. So Caracas became his ultimate destination, one million pounds became the amount he wanted, and the railway became the focus of the scheme he would develop for getting his hands on the cash – partly because it was so apt, and partly because it seemed to offer him the means by which to execute the plot beginning to take shape in his mind.

For the rest of the afternoon and the evening that followed, he continued to develop his plan, lying on the bed, marching up and down the room, or simply standing in the middle of it, motionless, as he wrestled with his thoughts. Whenever he thought of something new, he wrote it down, under one of a series of headings set out in the unused exercise book. By the time he went to bed that evening the plot was beginning to show definite promise and he had a list of things he needed to get and information he must find in order to ensure its success.

10

Week Three: Day Three –
On the Wednesday

On this day John's preparations began in earnest. The first thing he needed was information, and for that the internet was best. He also needed to create copies of all the papers in his possession: The Book of Excuses, the spreadsheet, his diaries and the Perma-way work order sheets. Embracing new technology in a way those who knew him would have found difficult to credit he decided that scanning and copying them onto compact discs was the best way of doing this. After breakfast, he set off for the town centre of South-newtown, where he was sure he would find what he wanted. He travelled by bus in order to avoid the CCTV system covering the railway network.

When he reached his destination he went first to the local branch of his bank and virtually emptied his current account of money; a not inconsiderable sum had built up over the years because his outgoings had almost always been less than his salary, and he had been too lazy to move the accumulated funds into a high-interest account. Then he visited the electrical mega-store where he was going to buy his computer.

For the first time John did not feel intimated by the assistants – who, in his opinion, did less in the way of assisting than they did in trying to make themselves look clever at the expense of their customers. As soon as John entered he was pounced on by one of these lads, who looked not much older than twelve.

'Good morning, sir,' said the twelve-year-old. 'Can I help you at all, or are you just browsing today?'

At least they've taught him some manners in whatever primary school he attends, John thought, but for 'browsing' read 'time-wasting'.

'I want to buy a laptop computer and a scanner, big enough to scan the pages of a book that is a little bigger than A4 size, so I suppose it will have to be A3. And then I want to be able to copy what I've scanned onto compact discs. Oh, yes, and I want to be able to connect to the internet. Do you have anything that can do all of that for me at a reasonable price?'

The assistant responded with an enthusiastic affirmative, then launched into techno-babble about RAMs, ROMs, caches, kilo-hertz, mega-bites, etc.

'Can I stop you there please sonny,' John said. 'You're speaking a language I don't understand. If I tell you exactly what I want it to do, can you tell me if you can sell me something that can do it?'

'I . . . I can try, sir,' the lad said, hesitancy creeping into his voice as he realised he was being asked to go 'off script'.

'I want to scan in several hundreds of pages, about a quarter of which are bigger than A4, but smaller than A3. Then I want to copy them onto three or four compact discs for storage, and I want to access the internet to search for information. Can you do that for me?'

'I . . . I think, I'd better fetch the manager.'

Eventually, the equipment he wanted was found to be in stock and called up from the storeroom. Having made sure he had sufficient compact discs, that he knew how to set up an account with an internet service provider and how to connect the equipment together without the need to take the twelve-year-old back to the hotel, he set about paying for it. This presented him with a whole new set of complications.

'How would you like to pay for this purchase, sir?' the cashier asked him.

'Cash, please,' he said. 'And do I get a discount for that?'

She looked at him as though he had demanded to spend a night of wanton passion with her mother. Cash was obviously seldom used in that store.

'I'll have to ask the manager.'

Is the manager the only one who knows anything in this place? thought John; and if I asked them that directly, would they need to ask the manager?

The manager arrived, expressed surprise at John's request and regretted that there was no possibility of his being offered a discount because the store already charged 'unbeatable rock-bottom prices'. Even then it was not over and done with because they wanted to know his name and address for 'their records' and to sell him an expensive three-year warranty plan. To the warranty the answer was a straight 'no': he thought it expensive and wondered why it should be considered necessary for a brand-new item of 'unsurpassed quality'. In any case, he did not anticipate using it for more than three days, let alone three years.

On the subject of his name and address, his first instinct was to refuse, but he decided that to argue was more trouble than it was worth, so he took a more pragmatic approach, calling himself Roland Smith and giving a fictitious address in the road where Pete lived. Then, at last, he was able to leave.

His next port of call was the mobile phone shop, to buy a pair of basic, pay-as-you-go phones. Here things were much simpler. The assistant was far less keen, and his lack of interest made John's task easier. John asked for what he wanted, the assistant got it, John handed over the cash, was given the two boxes in a plastic carrier bag, and away he went. There was no fuss about cash, there were no arguments about warranties, just a straightforward sale. The only thing he did insist on having was the assistant's assurance that both of the phones had the facility to block the sending of their numbers when they made a call, so that their users could remain anonymous – until they chose to reveal their identity by starting to speak.

Back at the hotel John connected his newly-acquired equipment and set it to work. His first task was to establish his internet connection, using the service provider Pete subscribed to. He had to make a phone call to the number provided to get a password that would allow him to download the software he needed. To do this he had to give the person on the other end his credit card details, something he was a little wary of doing, in case Adrian Wright and the agents of Arse could trace his whereabouts from it, but he quickly realised that his fear was almost certainly groundless. In the first place, as he knew from what Pete had told him, the service provider guarded the identity of its clients jealously, and in the second, all anyone monitoring credit card transactions would be able to find out was that he had spent money subscribing to that service, nothing more. The point of origin of the call would not be revealed as he was using a pay-as-you-go mobile phone – he had charged both up as soon as he had got back to his room.

Once connected to the internet, his first port of call was the website of Novice Airlines, to find out details of flights to Caracas. There were two flights a week, both leaving just after midday, one on Tuesday and one on Thursday. Thursday of that week was too soon, the Thursday of the following week too far away. It had to be the next Tuesday, his whole plan must be aimed at that day. There was a lot to think about and a lot to do. Once he had bought the tickets he would be committed, the time-frame would be set, and there would be no going back. As far as he could see, there were three ways of booking those tickets: he could do it on-line; he could do it on the phone; or he could do it in person, face-to-face with a member of Novice's staff in their sales office in Southnewtown. He chose the last method and made a mental note that the office opened at eight o'clock every morning.

With a definite time-scale to work to, he logged on to the website of the national train timetable, to begin the next part of his plan. He had no printer so he painstakingly wrote down the information he needed in the exercise book that was fast becoming the manual of his master plan. What he looked at were the times of trains on the London to Bigton main line, through North Downham, the airport and Bridges Junction; stopping services only, mainly going to and from Asham. As he compiled it, a clearer picture began to emerge and he saw that this plan was by no means fanciful; it was achieveable.

Later, when the pattern the pieces of his puzzle had made was almost complete, he logged out of the railway website and closed his internet connection. Then he settled down to begin scanning the pages of The Book of Excuses, the spreadsheet and his diaries, to the accompaniment of an old film on the television. A number of cups of tea and the complimentary biscuits the hotel provided kept him going until he went to the restaurant for his evening meal.

After dinner he drafted a letter to Angela, to be sent the following day. It did not take long. Most of what he wanted to say would be said on the phone when she rang him – if she rang him. Then he turned in for the night.

In the middle of a night during which he slept only fit-fully, the thought suddenly struck him that he had no idea how much space a million pounds would take up, how much it might weigh and whether he would be able to carry it – all rather important considering what he was about to attempt. Reluctantly, he got out of bed, settled down in front of the computer and logged on to the internet again. After a while he found a website about banknotes of all kinds from countries around the world, including the physical size of each of the notes issued by the Bank of England. Shortly afterwards he knew that used fifty-pound notes came in bundles of a thousand, each bundle being 159 millimetres long, 86 millimetres wide and 125 millimetres high. Twenty such bundles would be needed to make a million pounds; if these were stacked in five layers of four, they would occupy a space 318 millimetres long, 250 millimetres wide and 430 millimetres high – that was about 13 inches long, 10 inches wide and 18 inches high, about the size of a small suitcase. He worked out it would weigh 2.76 kilograms, well below the maximum allowance for hand baggage on Novice Airlines.

He next visited the website of one of the department stores he knew had a branch in Southnewtown and established that he could buy a hard-shelled suitcase a little bigger than the size of the stack of notes he intended to carry. His last port of call that day was a return to Novice Airlines, to check the allowance for carry-on hand luggage: a bag no more than 560 millimetres long, 230 millimetres wide and 360 millimetres high. This was slightly smaller than the bag he knew he would be carrying, but to a man about to attempt to blackmail a company that was part of the great British establishment, this hardly seemed to be important. What a profound change he had undergone! Formerly, the knowledge that his suitcase was marginally over the regulation size would have been a source of worry and lack of sleep. Now it did not even register. He went back to bed and slept soundly for the rest of the night.

11

Week Three: Day Four – On the Thursday

John looked long and hard at the unshaven face that stared back at him from the bathroom mirror. He had never had a beard before, and these first stages of its growth were unkempt, untidy and made him feel dirty.

After breakfast he left for the office of Novice Airlines. He arrived before it opened and waited outside, feeling conspicuous, but he had not long to wait. The young woman sitting behind the first desk he came to smiled at him as he approached.

'Good morning, sir,' she said. 'How can I help you?'

'I need to book two tickets for the flight to Caracas on Tuesday next week.'

'High Weald to Caracas, next Tuesday, two passengers. Would you like Super Class, Business, or Economy, sir?'

'I'm not quite sure about that,' John told her, 'but I do have some specific requirements. If I explain what they are, perhaps you can tell me what would be the best. I work for a small computer consultancy, not really a company as such, more a loose arrangement among a group of self-employed people. We've just landed a big contract in South America and two of us have to be out there on Wednesday to meet the clients and set up. The trouble is that one of the people we'd like to send is working in Germany at the moment, and if he doesn't finish what he's doing there in time, we might have to send someone else instead. Is it possible to book one ticket in the name of the person we know for certain will be going and one for another person, but leave the name until later?'

'I'm afraid not,' the girl told him. 'We need to have a name at the time of booking. But if you book into Super Class, you can change the details of that booking at no extra charge any time up to twelve hours before the flight is due to leave, including the passenger's name. You could book in the name of the person you think is likely to go, and change it later if you need to. Would that be OK?'

'That sounds ideal. If our man's not back from Germany twelve hours before the Caracas flight goes, he's hardly likely to be in the mood for going straight off again, particularly on a long-haul flight. That'll be fine.'

The girl turned back to the screen and began the process of booking two Super Class tickets. When she asked him for the names of the passengers, he gave Angela's first, then Pete's, with the intention of ringing in and changing it to his own at the last minute, so as to give Adrian Wright and his men as little opportunity as possible of stumbling across it, should they be able to monitor this kind of transaction. He had no idea whether or not they could, but it was better to be safe than sorry.

'Would it be possible for me to take Angela's ticket with me now, but leave the other one to be collected at the airport?

'Yes. In fact, it's the only way you can do it if you have to change the name at short notice. How would you like to pay?' she asked.

'Cash, if possible,' John replied, adding in response to her slightly quizzical look, for the sum involved was not small, 'I've just collected a fat fee from a rather eccentric client of ours. Because he knows a great deal about computers he has strong views on their level of security. He refuses to use banks and insists that all his dealings, with us and everyone else, be in cash.'

John marvelled at what an accomplished liar he was becoming. He handed over the cash, collected Angela's ticket and left.

His next port of call was the post office, where he bought a few envelopes, some sheets of brown paper and a book of first-class stamps.

Retiring to a convenient table, he wrapped in brown paper the box containing the mobile phone he had bought for Angela. 'Do not open this until you have read the letter in the envelope numbered 1', he wrote neatly on each of its sides. Next he put the airline ticket in one of the envelopes, sealed it and wrote on the outside: 'This is envelope number 2. Do not open it until you have read the letter in envelope number 1'. Then he settled down to the part of the exercise that he was least sure about, the letter to Angela.

'Dear Angela', he wrote, copying from the draft he had made the night before, 'This will probably come as something of a surprise to you but not, I hope, an unpleasant one. I have to go away for a time – perhaps even permanently – and I want you to come with me, so that we can share a new life together. I realise now this is something that I/we should have done a very long time ago and I hope you will forgive me for not asking you before and agree with me that it is never too late. I hope you will come. I have made most of the arrangements and sent you a plane ticket in the hope that you will. We leave next Tuesday on the 12:05 p.m. Novice Airlines flight to Caracas. I am sorry I cannot see you at the moment to ask you in person – I will explain later why that is. Please think very hard about this and please, please come with me. As well as the ticket, I have also sent you a mobile phone. You can use it to contact me if you want, or need, to – my new number is written at the bottom of this letter. Please do not try my old number.

I am not using it any more. And please, please do not go round to my house. I am not there at the moment and it might not be safe for either of us if you did. Again, that is something I cannot explain at the moment, but I will when we meet – if we meet. If you decide to come, go to the airport, check in and get on the plane. I will catch up with you when I have finished all the arrangements I am having to make. Don't worry if I cut it a bit fine – I *will* be there. And it would probably be for the best if you did not tell anyone about any of this whether you decide to come or not. Please do. I am relying on it.

Yours, in hope. John.'

At the bottom he wrote the number of his new phone. He read and re-read the letter several times over, his confidence waxing and waning as he did so. First he convinced himself that she would want to come, then that there was no reason on earth why she possibly could. Eventually, tired of his own indecision, he folded the sheet of paper and sealed it in an envelope: for better or for worse. After writing on the outside: 'Envelope 1 – open and read first', he put it on top of the other envelope on top of the mobile phone box, and wrapped them all in a second sheet of brown paper, sealing the parcel with copious amounts of the sticky tape he had brought with him from the hotel. He wrote Angela's address on the outside, carried it to the counter and despatched it first class.

Now, he thought as he left the building, I'm truly committed and there's no going back.

Out in the sunshine again, he headed for the central bus station, stopping on the way in a luggage and accessory shop to buy himself a baseball cap, not something he would ever have considered owning or wearing in his former life, and the small suitcase in which he planned to deposit a million pounds in used fifties. This action made the whole enterprise seem unreal again, as he felt there was no way that he, John Biddle, could ever own such a sum.

Carrying the old suitcase with The Book, the spreadsheet and the diaries inside, and pulling along behind him the new, small case with its little wheels and extending handle for towing, he walked to the central bus station, where he boarded a bus to the airport. Before alighting he forced himself to don the baseball cap, in the hope that its peak would help to cover his face when he passed any CCTV cameras.

He got off in front of the main terminal building and made his way to where the concourse crossed the main London to Bigton railway line, above the station. Here a line of large, plate-glass windows looked northwards along the tracks, with rows of seats facing them. John sat down, one eye on his watch and the other on the railway lines; he stayed there until each of the trains he was interested in had passed, marking them off on the copy of the timetable he had written out and brought with him, specifically for that purpose. When he had finished, he returned to the main terminal building and found a bank of left-luggage lockers. He hired one for himself and locked his new suitcase inside it, on the bottom shelf.

On his way back to the hotel he got off the bus at The Boltons and walked, choosing a route that took him the wrong way, towards a place he had seen on a map on the internet the night before, where a footbridge spanned the railway. Having made sure there were no cameras in the vicinity, he climbed the stairs and walked out into the centre of the bridge, knowing that this was a safe place from which to observe the movement of the trains when he needed to. He stayed there for a while and watched a few go past, his mood swinging between exhilaration and doubt about what he was planning, until he decided it was time to return to the hotel and scan some more documents.

By the evening, after another long session in front of the computer, the scanning was complete. John then copied all the scanned documents onto three compact discs: one for him to take with him, one for a solicitor with whom he intended to leave everything except The Book of Excuses, and one to send to Stephen Dent, as part of his insurance policy against future harm, and to show him he was serious. He also recorded a voice massage on each disc, describing its contents, what it was for and where it had come from.

His last task that day was to prepare the package for the solicitor – really two packages, one inside the other. The inner one contained the pile of paper that was the spread-sheet, his railway diaries and the folder of Perma-way papers, plus a copy of the disc. The outer one contained a letter with instructions that if John did not make contact at reg-ular intervals to verify his safety, the solicitor was to release the inner package to the news media via a well-known image/media consultant, who would know exactly what to do with it. John wrapped it all up in the last of the brown paper he had bought and put it on the desk to be dealt with in the morning.

12

Week Three: Day Five – On the Friday

The electronic alarm on John's watch sounded unduly loud when it went off at three o'clock in the morning. John sat up in bed and turned it off, then picked up his mobile phone. He punched in a number, lifted the phone to his ear and waited. It rang for only a short while before it was answered by a brusque and businesslike voice that snapped 'Yes.'

'Hello Adrian', John said quietly, trying to convey a sense of confidence and control that in reality he did not feel. 'Have I woken you up, or are you having trouble sleeping these days?'

'Don't start trying to pull my chain, Biddle: you're causing me . . . us, a great deal of trouble. What is it you want?'

'I think you can probably guess the answer to that: I want to trade.'

'You want to trade.'

'If you're just going to repeat everything I say, this is going to be very tiresome and take us a very long time. I want to trade. You know what I have. I wonder what it might be worth to you and the people who pull your strings.'

'Don't try to be clever, Biddle. Leave that to those who are good at it.'

'Clever, Adrian?' John said with a laugh. 'You have no idea where I am; you don't have your beloved book; and right now you have no idea when, or even whether, you're going to get it back. What's so clever about that?'

'Tell me what you want,' Wright said, refusing to rise to the bait.

' OK. I want a million pounds – in used fifty-pound notes.'

There was silence at the other end of the line.

'Did you hear me Adrian?'

'I heard you all right. You're joking, aren't you? You can't seriously think we're going to give that sort of money to some jumped-up, get-lucky amateur who happened to find himself in the right place at the right time and managed to grab himself a copy of a dusty old book!'

'I don't think you've got a lot of choice, Adrian. Lucky or not, I've got the book. I've also got a few other things that are telling me loud and clear what the Perma-way directors and their pals at Roamer-Phone have been up to.'

John heard a sharp intake of breath at the other end of the line at his mention of the involvement of the mobile phone company.

'You've gone quiet, Adrian. Have I surprised you? Did you think I wouldn't be able to work it out? I've got all the evidence I need. I've seen the figures – I've got copies of them right here. I know how much it's all been worth and, believe me, they can afford it. I wonder how the travelling public would react if they were to read in their morning papers over breakfast one day – or even better, if they read it while they were stuck on a train somewhere – that most of the delays they've been forced to put up with for who knows how many years have been artificially created, just to line the pockets of a few immoral fat-cats. There'd be blood spilled at stations all over the country.'

There was a long silence.

Eventually, John broke it. 'Do we have a deal?'

'I can't say. I'll have to consult.'

'Well you'd better be quick about it', because I want the money next week.'

'When, next week?' Wright asked.

'I don't know yet: I haven't decided, but I'll let you know when I have. Get the money, Adrian, or the whole thing goes public. When I get the money, you get the book; then everyone's happy. I'll be in touch.'

He clicked off the phone, let his arm drop, and sank back onto the bed.

Later on in the morning, having tried and having failed to get back to sleep, John left the hotel and walked to where the footbridge crossed the railway tracks and he could watch the trains go by. As each one streamed along the tracks under his feet he marked it off on his copy of the timetable, noting how well they were running to time – again.

How strange, he thought sarcastically, that now I have their Book of Excuses, the trains should suddenly start to run so well to time. They must be finding it hard to think of reasons for them to be late, and their income must have dropped dramatically too: no need for all those 'Hello, it's me; I'm on a train' phone calls.

When he had seen the trains he was most interested in go by, John left the bridge and walked back to the main road, where he took a bus to North Downham. On the way there it passed through the long, strung-out suburb that flanked the road on both sides, with rows of semi-detached houses punctuated by parades of shops like those around the Army Surplus store. One in particular caught his attention.

When he got off he set about finding a firm of solicitors. He did not know why he had come to North Downham specifically, because there were solicitors' offices to be found all over. Perhaps he just wanted a change of scene from Southnewtown, or perhaps he thought his chances of being spotted by the agents of Arse were greater if he kept returning to the same place. He supposed there would be more solicitors to choose from in Downham, because it was a more affluent area, not that he knew how he would choose one, but he had a vague feeling he would know which was the right one when he found it.

Most of the solicitors seemed to have chosen to congregate in a small area of the town, comprising just a few streets. After walking up and down for a while, examining their fronts and peering through office windows, he allowed his innate conservatism to guide him, and entered a staid-looking premises of Dickensian appearance that spoke to him of tradition and trust. The name plate read 'Everest and Goodbody'. Its interior did not belie the impression given by the frontage, and he was pleased to see the receptionist was an older lady of comfortable aspect.

'Good morning, dear,' she said. 'Can I help you?'

'Would it be possible to speak to a solicitor, please?'

'Do you have an appointment?'

'No. Do I need one?'

'Not always. Let me go and see if our Mr Everest is available.'

She stood up, struggled across to a door at the back of the office, knocked, went in, and pushed it closed behind her. John heard muffled voices, then the receptionist emerged and asked him if he would like to go in.

Mr Everest was a substantial, grey-haired, elderly man, whose size, in every dimension, suited his name. When John entered the musty confines of his office he was sitting behind his desk, in a high-backed leather chair. He did not rise to shake hands, and John guessed it might well be because he would have found it difficult to do so. His welcome, however, was warm enough.

'Good day, sir, good day. Come in and take a seat. I am William Everest, the senior partner in the firm of Everest and Goodbody: the only partner in the firm of Everest and Goodbody, in fact. I'll be honest with you from the start of our business relationship – assuming we're to have one, of course – I work here alone, with only my secretary, Margaret, for company. There is no Goodbody here – only this one . . . ' and as he said it he patted both hands on his waistcoat front, and laughed loudly at his own joke. 'Now, what can I do for you, Mr . . . um . . . ?'

John was quiet for a second, then began slowly. 'I'd prefer if I could keep my name a secret – for personal reasons.'

'Intriguing,' said Mr Everest. 'So how shall we identify you? In such situations I normally suggest that we name you according to the town you come from and the person that you most despise. Mr Town-hyhen-Person. OK? Which makes you?'

'Mr Asham-Smythe,' John replied, after a moment's thought.

'Excellent, excellent. A name that conveys a sense of both quality and dignity. Are you related to the Asham Asham-Smythes at all?' He laughed again. 'Now, what can I do for you, Mr Asham-Smythe?'

'I have a package I want to leave in your care, for an indefinite period of time. I want you to keep it for me, unopened, for as long as I contact you regularly to let you know I am still happy, healthy and, above all, alive.'

'You intrigue me more and more, Mr Asham-Smythe. May I be permitted to ask what is in your mysterious package?'

'That's something I'd prefer not to tell anyone, for reasons of *their* safety, as well as mine.'

'Just so, and as you will. I'm to keep this package for you, and you'll contact me from time to time to let me know that you are hale and hearty. How will I know it's you I'm speaking to?'

John had not considered this, but he realised at once that it was a wise precaution. He began thinking out loud.

'Firstly, we two are the only ones who know my new identity. That could be the starting point. Beyond that, perhaps we should have some kind of password; one that changes every time we make contact.'

'Yes, yes,', Everest cried enthusiastically. 'We should change the password whenever we speak, so the conversation we have each time will begin with the password we agreed the last time we spoke, and end with the selection of the new word for the next time. With your permission I would like to volunteer to be the person who selects those passwords.'

'Of course,' John said. 'That would be fine.'

'Excellent! This is excellent. Like playing at spies, or being a character in a James Bond film. How often will you contact me?'

'Once a month – to begin with – perhaps on the first of each month.'

'Make it the *last* day of each month. I make a point of being here on the last few days of every month as there's always a lot to be done at month-end.'

'That's agreed then,' John said. 'How much will you charge me for this service?'

'My dear boy,' Everest replied, 'like so many in my dry and dusty profession I have spent all of my working life waiting for a day like this. Then you cross my threshold with your package and your mysterious story. You strike me as an honest and straightforward man, so how could I charge you for the honour of being a part of this . . . adventure – provided you promise that one day you will tell me what it's all about.'

'I will, when the time's right,' John told him. 'You have my word on it.'

'Splendid,' exclaimed Everest. 'Now I need to know what you would require of me in the unfortunate event that you are unable to make the contact we've agreed.'

'The package has been wrapped twice. It has two layers. Between the two there's an envelope, containing a letter that will give you your instructions. The inner package contains information, in the form of documents and a compact disc, to be run on a computer, that would be very damaging to a number of people and an important organisation were it to become common knowledge. If I don't make contact as we've agreed, or within, say, ten days of a date when I should have made contact, you are to see that this information does become common knowledge. To do that you will need to open the outer wrapping and read the letter. Then you'll know what all this is about. The inner package you should take to Cliff Maxford, the media publicist, or whoever has assumed his rôle if he's no longer on the scene, or no longer the best person of his type to consult. At that point you'll be able to claim full payment for your efforts because, if I'm no longer around, you can allow Mr Maxford to negotiate whatever he can get for the contents of the package, and keep the proceeds for yourself, or dispose of them as you see fit.'

'Thank you. That's most kind of you,' said Everest, more out of good manners than gratitude because, for all he knew, the contents might be worthless. 'Now, is there anything else I can do for you?'

'I'd like to open a numbered Swiss bank account – one of those you read about in books, the ones that are secret and to which no-one but the owner can gain access. They do exist, don't they?' he asked anxiously.

'Yes, Mr Asham-Smythe, I can confirm that they do, and it shouldn't be any trouble to open one on your behalf. I'll give you the details when we next speak.'

'Thank you,' said John, 'and I *will* pay you for your work, so you must tell me how much I owe. Then I'll find a way to get the money to you.'

'That's most kind, but we'll debate that point when there's something to talk about.'

'Well, that's it really,' said John, 'other than to give you this.' He reached down to the suitcase on the floor beside his chair, took out the package and put it on Everest's desk. 'You will take good care of it, won't you?'

'I most certainly will. You may rest assured on that point. As soon as we're finished here, I'll personally take it to my bank and place it in the safe depository I have on hire there for my most valuable papers and artefacts. There it will stay until you instruct me otherwise – in whatever manner.'

John shut the suitcase and stood up. Everest shook his hand and wished him good luck in a very formal way, then showed him out through both doors into the street.

On the bus back to The Boltons, John consulted the timetable of events he had planned and the list of what he needed. His destination how was the Army Surplus Store near the station. He got off on the pavement outside the shop and went in.

He was the only customer. A man John assumed was the proprietor sat on a stool behind the counter reading a newspaper. It was very quiet, all sound being deadened by the numerous military-style garments hanging from racks, rails and hooks all around the walls. John began by searching the racks of jackets for something that would make him look inconspicuous and had many pockets, some of them with zips. He found it in a rack labelled 'the espionage range'. Not exactly inconspicuous, as it was red on one side and pale blue on the other, it was, however, reversible, which was better, and had pockets galore, all of them with zips. It was a little too big for him but would suit his purpose for the short period of time he would be wearing it. He also found a pair of tough and durable gloves, made from a fabric thin enough to allow much of the sense of feeling to be retained in fingers and palms. Next he selected a light fabric bag, in which to carry The Book of Excuses and the other items he would need when he and Wright met. For the next fifteen or twenty minutes, he searched without success until the man behind the counter looked up from his paper and said,

'Can I help at all?'

John decided that to get what he wanted he was going

to have to trust him.

'I'm looking for a few things I need for a ... um ... project I'm about to undertake,' he said. 'But I can't see them anywhere on the shelves or racks.'

'We have more ... er ... specialised items available for private viewing in the rooms at the back,' the man told him. 'What is it you're looking for?'

John hesitated, not knowing the correct terminology, then decided to describe the things in his own words, rather than try to be clever.

'A smoke bomb,' he said, 'and a device for cutting off or jamming mobile phone signals. They're for ...'

'Please don't,' the man interrupted, holding his hands out in front of him, palms towards his customer. 'You don't need to tell me and I don't need to know – even if what you were about to tell me was a cover story for what you're really doing. What I have here is all legal at the point of sale. Whether it stays that way is entirely the responsibility of the buyer and is nothing to do with me. Let me shut up shop, then I'll take you through.'

He walked to the door and shot home the bolts at top and bottom. Then he spun the sign in the window round to read 'closed' and led John through to the rooms at the back of the shop. The first one contained racks and shelves of cardboard boxes of various sizes, marked only with numbers – no words or pictures to indicate their contents.

'There's a variety of smoke bombs here,' the proprietor told John, 'from ones meant only for small rooms to larger ones for areas outdoors. What is it you want?'

'A small one,' John told him.

The man plucked a box from one of the shelves, opened it and tipped out onto his hand a dull grey metal cylinder, slightly bigger than a woman's lipstick. A metal ring was attached to one end.

'Hold it at this end, hook a finger through the ring, and

pull off the top. Throw the cylinder where you want it to go and presto! Instant smoke. Alternatively, if you've only got one hand free, clench the ring between your teeth, pull, and away you go. OK?'

John pictured its use. 'That sounds ideal.'

The man led him into the next room, selected a box from another shelf, opened it and slid out onto his palm a black plastic container about the size of a small spectacle case.

'Mobile phone signal jammer. Takes two standard double-A-sized batteries. Range about a hundred metres. Battery life switched on is about three days. Two recessed buttons to operate it, one for on, one for off. Small, red LED lights up to confirm that it's on, but that can be taped over for operations in blackout conditions. It's very popular with restaurant-goers who want to be able to eat undisturbed by other people's noisy phone calls.'

John stared at the device in awe, doing a quick calculation of distance in his head to satisfy himself that the range was long enough. Then he looked around at the boxes stacked on either side of him. Unlike those in the previous room, these advertised their contents loudly, in both pictures and words. One of the displays on his left-hand side caught his eye, and he knew that he needed what was in that box, too. He picked it up for a closer look.

'That's a new product,' the proprietor told him. 'Only recently launched. It blocks off signals from global positioning satellites, so your opponents' GPS trackers won't work any more – the downside is that neither do yours. Similar range, performance and operation to the phone jammer. Sized to fit easily into a pocket, too.'

'I'll take both of them,' John said without hesitation.

The proprietor slid the phone jammer back into its box and closed it, then moved on into the next room, which looked like a small arsenal: rack upon rack of guns, from small pistols to huge automatic rifles that looked as though they could stop an advancing army.

'Need any replica weapons for your . . . um . . . project?'

'They're replicas?' John asked.

'Yep, each and every one of 'em. I can't stock the real things: probably wouldn't want to either. But these can be just as useful if you need to persuade people.'

John had not thought about arming himself before, but he could see the advantages of having one of these, even the smallest of them, if Wright arse proved to be difficult. He would not want to hurt him – well, OK, he would; but not seriously. He walked up and down the racks, staring hard at what he judged to be very convincing replicas. He had never seen the real things, so he was in no position to judge, but . . . he stopped in front of a rack holding what looked like automatic pistols – small, compact, secret agent-style guns. He reached out.

'OK if I try one out for size?' he asked.

'Be my guest.'

It was heavier than he had expected, and cold against his skin. He weighed it in his left hand, then in his right. It felt comfortable and reassuring. He held it out at arm's length, as though aiming at the far end of the room, and knew he could not resist the feeling of confidence and power it gave him – power over Wright Arse, his adversary, his enemy.

'I'll take this, too,' he said quietly.

The two men returned to the front of the shop and John paid for his purchases, using most of what remained of his cash. When everything had been loaded and taped into plain, brown paper bags and dropped into the suitcase on top of The Book of Excuses, he set out to walk back to the hotel, feeling different again now that he was armed with the weapons of war – and almost ready to declare it.

13

Weekend Three

In spite of everything John had been through and was planning to put himself through in the days that were to come, he could not help feeling self-conscious on Saturday morning as he approached the shop that called itself Fetishica. The dummies in the window could see him; everyone in the neighbourhood could see him; he could even see himself, reflected in the window glass, and they all knew – or thought they knew – why he was going there. He alone knew the real reason, but there was no way he could tell anyone. He paused outside the door, took a deep breath, swallowed hard and went in. Like the Army Surplus Store along the road, the interior of Fetishica was most definitely a world apart, and whereas what he had seen in the other shop were things he had either seen before or found it easy to imagine, what he saw in this one were things he had never seen before and were chiefly beyond his imagination. It was quiet inside Fetishica, the noise deadened by the fabric of the clothing and outfits hanging from racks and rails around its walls: items in leather, items in rubber, outfits of all types that hung and clung, outfits that revealed more than they covered or covered everything they could for the sake of mystery and anonymity, uniforms and costumes of all shapes and sizes. In between the clothes were racks and cabinets of 'equipment', from simple whips, chains, ropes and handcuffs to more complicated items with spikes and studs, or electrical 'toys' whose purpose he did not care to guess at.

If this place has rooms out the back, he thought, I have no desire to visit them. The thought of what might be found there frightens me to death . . . and bloody hell, so does that!

'That' was the shop assistant he had just caught sight of in the corner of the room, a person of indeterminate sex, its face covered in gaudy make-up and almost every visible feature pierced with a ring or stud of some kind, linked together by chains. It had long hair, dyed like some kind of faded rainbow, hanging limply round its face and shoulders, shoulders that were covered by what looked like a cross between a set of black motor-cycle leathers and a bright orange kaftan – a piece at clothing as shapeless and unattractive as the person wearing it. It looked up from the paperback book it was reading.

'Are you OK, or is there something I can help you with?' it said in a voice that did nothing to help him decide what its gender might be.

'No, I'm OK at the moment,' John replied. 'Just looking.'

His instinct was to run out of the place but he resisted and knuckled down to the task of finding what he had come in for. He looked slowly around, picturing the scenario he was planning, playing it through in his head, knowing he would recognise what he was seeking when he came across it. He was right; he reached up and took it from the hook where it hung. He was examining it for some indication of size when he heard a voice at his shoulder.

'That's a very good choice. A very popular outfit, that one is,' the assistant said quietly, in a tone that made John's flesh creep. 'Is it for you, or for someone else?'

'It's a present . . . for someone else, a friend . . . a sort of joke present. I was just looking for a label to tell me what size it is.'

'Let me,' said the assistant, leaning across him to take the hanger from his grasp.

'How big is the person it's meant for?'

'About the same size as me, I suppose,' John replied, before he had time to think what he was saying.

A knowing smile crossed the assistant's face. It was the oldest story in the book.

'I think it's a large one,' it said, holding the item out and sizing it against John's body, looking him up and down appraisingly. John was now feeling very uncomfortable indeed. He had broken out in a sweat. The assistant's next words did nothing to alleviate his discomfort.

'You can try it on if you like. If you and your 'friend' are about the same size and it fits you, then it'll fit him, too. The fitting room's out the back. Let me know if you need any help. I'll gladly give you a hand.'

'N. . . n. . . no thanks,' John stammered. 'It's OK. I'm sure it'll be OK. I'll take it as it is.'

'All right, but it's your loss if it doesn't fit,' the assistant told him, turning away down the shop towards the till. 'If you find it doesn't fit when you get it home, we can't change it, you know.'

John still wanted to run away, but he couldn't, until he had paid for the outfit. He tried to relax and convince himself that his virtue was not under threat, that this was just idle banter to brighten up an otherwise boring day. Besides, he needed something else as well: something that was only going to make things worse. As he followed the assistant, he picked up a pair of handcuffs and took them with him.

At the till, the assistant looked at the label on the outfit and tapped its price on the keyboard. John held out the handcuffs.

'Are these strong enough to keep someone restrained, or are they just for playing games with?' he asked, dreading (and receiving) the knowing smile and twinkle in the eye of the assistant.

'Why don't you give them a try?' Taking the handcuffs and one of John's wrists, it brought the two together with some force to clamp the metal bracelet closed around the wrist before John could snatch it away. 'There. Try that.'

John tugged hard at the cold metal encircling his wrist, but managed to do nothing more than chafe the skin. He decided it would do.

'Would you like the other one put on too?' the assistant asked, 'Just to see if you like it.'

'No thanks,' John said quickly. 'I think they'll do. I'll take them, and the . . . um, outfit. Now could you find the key and release me, please.'

' OK,' the assistant said, sounding disappointed.

A few minutes later John was back outside, his purchases shut away in his suitcase. He was rather glad he had brought the suitcase with him because the bag in which his purchases had been put had the name of the shop emblazoned across it in large letters, with a rather graphic picture underneath depicting something the dummies in the window might have got up to. Did anyone, he wondered, ever come here and walk away swinging one of these bags merrily by their side? Or did they bring their own, unmarked bags with them?

From the sex shop, John headed for The Boltons station. His next two tasks involved the railway. The first of these was to take possession of one of the lockers on the station platform provided for cyclists to store their bikes while making a train journey. He had no bike, but had other uses in mind and wanted to secure one early to make that he had one when he needed it. It was also a reasonably secure place to leave his suitcase, carrying it would hamper what he was about to attempt. When he had found a locker and stowed his suitcase, he awaited the arrival of the first train heading north.

Expressed in words, John's second task involving the railway was quite a simple one. In practice, however, it was considerably harder and carried a large element of risk, but it was essential to the plan he had developed, and could not be avoided. When the next northbound train arrived, he boarded it and settled into a seat from where he could observe the actions of the guard, taking note of what he did at and between the stations they stopped at as they made their way up the line towards Suburbia and London. Not wanting to go all the way into London, and not yet having had the opportunity to do what he needed to do, he got off at South Suburbia and crossed over to one of the down platforms to wait for a train going south. He tried to look inconspicuous and keep out of view of the cameras. The next train arrived and he got on, again taking a seat from where he could watch the guard.

His chance did not come on that train, nor on the one he took going north again to South Suburbia when he changed at the airport, hoping to stay lost among the crowds there. The opportunity he sought finally came on the next journey south, on a train heading for Asham. As soon as they stopped at the first station out of South Suburbia he knew that this train was the one he had been waiting for. The guard, instead of staying on board and leaning out of his open doorway to look along its length, was one of those who liked to get off and walk to the back of each platform they stopped at to get a better view of the doors of his train. That left his control panel unattended for a short time at each station.

John watched the guard work at the next few stops, making sure he knew the man's routine. It was invariably the same: open the doors, get off and walk forward to the back edge of the platform, then stand facing the train, looking right and left along its length. When everyone who wanted to had got off or on, he would walk forward and get back on himself, then press the button to close all the doors except his own. Finally, he would close his and press the signal button four times to tell the driver it was safe to move off.

When John was ready, he walked towards the doors, positioning himself a short way behind the guard as the train slowed down for its next stop, Lord's Copse, a station to the north of The Boltons. He could feel his anxiety levels rising with every second, his heart was beating faster, he had a sick feeling in his stomach and a strong urge to run away. But he was made of sterner stuff than he realised and he stayed put, waiting for the train to stop. It slowed; it slowed; it stopped. The guard pressed the button to open the doors. He stepped onto the platform. John stepped forward behind him, as if to do the same thing. The guard walked the several paces it took him to cross the width of the platform and began to turn. Meanwhile, John stepped forward to the threshold and grabbed the bunch of keys hanging from the slot in the control panel. His heart was in his mouth as he stepped onto the platform, sliding the keys into his trouser pocket. He glanced at the guard as the guard turned to look at him, having been staring down the platform at the back of the train when John stepped out. John walked past him, towards the station exit, fighting down an almost irresistible urge to break into a run before the guard tried to close the doors, using a control panel that would not now work because it had been turned off and there were no keys to turn it back on again. He walked out through the opening in the high brick wall supporting the back of the canopy roof over the platform and instinctively turned to the right, because he had seen that the ground sloped quickly downwards there and he would drop out of sight at the foot of the embankment onto which the line emerged from the station's southern end.

As he turned the corner and was no longer visible from the train, he broke into a run. He ran along the length of the wall behind the platform, down the slope at the foot of the embankment, across the road that ran under the railway line beyond the end of the station, and onto a footpath that disappeared into a wood. Even then he did not stop. On the far side of the wood the path emerged into an open area of ground skirting the edge of a huge construction site, where a massive, old building was being converted into luxury apartments. This, he knew, was the old North Downs Lunatic Asylum, a private establishment originally built in Victorian times to house insane gentlefolk. In the old days, you had to be mad and rich to live there. Now, with the prices developers would be charging for their 'exclusive', 'executive' conversions, you would have to be both mad and rich to live there once more.

Beyond the building site there was another road leading to the more modern, general hospital. John, by now all but done-in by the unaccustomed exercise, decided to head for it, seeing there the opportunity to rest and blend in with the crowd, just in case he was being pursued. Before he did so, he slipped out of the jacket he was wearing, and took off his baseball cap and sunglasses, to alter his appearance slightly. It was not much, but it could do him no harm.

He slowed his pace to a fast walk; no need to draw attention to himself by rushing. In one hand he carried the tightly-balled jacket, his hat and sunglasses, in the other, buried deep in his trouser pocket, he clutched the bunch of keys from the train. When the path reached the hospital building he followed the signs into the Accident and Emergency Department and took a seat at the back of the waiting area, apparently just another red-faced, somewhat breathless, distressed-looking person amongst a sea of others. It was an ideal place to hide while he recovered from the uncomfortable exercise he had just subjected himself to. The chair he took was not uncomfortable; the atmosphere was warm and soporific; John was tired after his exertions, but the adrenalin that still coursed through his body would not let him fall asleep. For an hour or so he watched people come and go; he read the notices on the walls, then a newspaper a patient had left behind on the seat next to him. Eventually he got up and went outside, fully prepared to make a run for it if necessary. It was not necessary: there was no-one in sight who resembled a railway official or a policeman – only patients, relatives, visitors, ambulance men and taxi-drivers.

John took a taxi from the hospital back to his hotel. Back in his room he was restored to calm and to safety. He wished he could have stayed there, behind its locked door, but he knew he had to go out again to collect his suitcase from the locker, something he would not feel safe doing until after dark. Other than that he had simply to wait: for Tuesday to come; for Angela to ring him, if indeed she was going to – or for the agents of Arse to come bursting through the door with their weapons drawn, or even blazing. None of those things happened. The trip to the station was uneventful, and John returned feeling rather bored.

Sunday was a day when there was nothing he had to do, and it did nothing for him. To improve his mood he bought a paper, and read it through from cover to cover; then he settled down to run through his plan from start to finish, laying out the things he had bought and would be needing, and making yet another list of the things he still had to do before he would be ready.

In the evening he tried to phone Angela but got no answer from the mobile phone he had sent her, only the answering service. He left a message, perhaps more for him than for her, because after he had said what he had to say he knew there was no more he could do, and the decision as to whether she would go with him or not was entirely hers.

'Hello, Angela. It's John', he said. 'I hope you got my letter and the phone I sent you: of course, if you didn't then you wouldn't be listening to this so that's quite a stupid thing to say, but you know me: always ready with some stupid comment or other, whatever the occasion. I just wanted to say in person what I said in the letter: I'm off to start a new life on Tuesday and I want you to come with me. I realise now that we should have been together for a long time, and we've missed lots of chances in life, and I don't want us to miss this one too. So please come. That's all really: please come. I hope I'll see you on Tuesday. Bye.'

It sounded stupid and ineffectual. He put down the phone, turned off the light, and tried to sleep.

14

Week Four: Day One – Monday

The next morning he was up and about early as this was the day when everything started in earnest. Breakfast with his suitcase by his side was followed by a swift walk to the footbridge over the railway to watch the trains for the last time. He satisfied himself that everything was still running more or less to schedule, as The Book of Excuses was still missing and whatever Perma-way might have intended to replace it with was obviously not ready. He was also able to confirm that the services using the new trains the week before were still using them that day and, therefore, by extension, would be that week; those employing the old slam-door stock were also still the same. Knowing that had become essential to the execution of his plan.

When he had seen enough he left the bridge and caught the bus into Southnewtown. Here he visited a pet shop – to buy a rat. The shop had quite a range of these rodents. Many were white, and most were small. They were not what John had in mind, but at the far end of the row of cages he found exactly what he wanted: a pair of bigger rats, both brown in colour, sharing the same cage.

'You'll do', he told them. 'You'll do very nicely, and I hope you'll enjoy your freedom when you get it – if you manage to escape what lies ahead of you. Some minutes later he left the shop, his two purchases housed in a brand new carrying-cage. 'I'll be sorry to see them go really,' the assistant said as he paid. 'They've been quite good company. They're very bright, always nosing around to see what's going on. They didn't sell when they were babies – the kids all want white ones, not brown – and now they've grown they're too big to be cute and cuddly so no-one wants them. Except you, that is. It's nice to know they'll be going to a good home.'

'If only you knew,' John thought, 'you wouldn't be so happy.'

Leaving the shop, John also carried a plastic bag containing a small food bowl, a packet of rat food and a large water bottle. He walked into the nearby public park and sat down on the first unoccupied bench he came to and emptied the contents of the carrier bag onto the seat beside him. He opened the bag of food, filled up the bowl, put the bowl in the cage with the rats and dropped the rest into the waste bin that stood at the end of the bench. He assembled the water bottle, then lifted the cage into the carrier bag and walked across the grass to the public toilet on the far side of the park, where he filled the bottle from the only working tap he could find in the place, and attached it to the side of the cage. The rats now had food and water; they would not die before he needed them. The food bowl was not very big, so they might go hungry towards the end, but the water bottle was large, and they would need to drink more than they needed to eat. If they were hungry they were more likely to run about when given their freedom, which would suit his purpose very well.

From the park, John walked back to the bus station and took a bus to the airport. He donned his baseball cap and sunglasses which, along with his new growth of beard, made him look very different from the John Biddle of old and would, he hoped, render him unrecognisable to Adrian Wright Arse and the collection of Arse men who would undoubtedly be somewhere behind him when the build-up to the exchange began on the morning of the next day.

At the airport, John entered the terminal building. Inside, he went straight to the left luggage locker he was using and deposited the cage with its rodent occupants inside. Then, carrying the old suitcase he had taken almost everywhere with him for the last week, he strolled around the inside of the terminal building, trying to look like any other traveller with time to kill before checking in for a flight. Instead of checking in, however, he checked out where everything was inside the building, so that his arrival the following day would be as smooth and uneventful as he hoped it would be.

When he had had a good look round he returned to his hotel for the last time.

The hours of the afternoon and evening passed slowly, giving him plenty of time to prepare and far too much time to think. His preparation was methodical. First he went through the plan he had developed, step by step, collecting on the bed everything he would need, and placing on the desk against the far wall all the things he knew he would not. Then he arranged all the items on the bed in the order they would be needed, from foot to head. First there was the reversible jacket, which he would wear red side out to begin with. He laid it at the foot of the bed, having first unzipped all its pockets and made sure they were empty. Then there was his new mobile phone, the key to the bike locker on The Boltons station, the gloves, the phone jammer, the GPS jammer, the smoke bomb and the gun, all of which he took time and pains to wipe clean of all trace of his fingerprints; followed by The Book of Excuses, the two remaining copies of the computer discs and the bag he had bought for The Book and other bits and pieces. After that came the carrier bag with the outfit he had bought from Fetishica, then the handcuffs, the keys he had stolen from the train guard, the key to the left luggage locker at the airport, and finally his passport. He stared down at this odd collection of articles laid out along the edge of the bed, simultaneously excited by what they represented and what he was about to attempt to do with them, while at the same time awed by the thought that it was he, and not the hero of some paperback novel he might have read on a train, who was about to attempt it all.

After a while he picked up the jacket and slipped it on, his determination renewed to pay Wright Arse and Perma-way back for what they had done to him, both recently and over all the years of delay and frustration he had endured on their trains. One by one he picked up the articles on the bed, stowing them in various pockets of the jacket or in the Army Surplus bag, as appropriate. He was careful to pick up with his handkerchief everything he had just cleaned so meticulously. One of the computer discs went into a pocket; the other into an envelope he addressed to Stephen Dent at his Perma-way office, along with a note telling him to ask Adrian Wright to explain it to him. The last item was the bunch of keys he had taken from the train. He only needed one of these, but he kept them all just in case, having made absolutely sure he knew which was the one he needed and could find it easily, even if he was in a tearing hurry.

Next he sorted out the clothes he would be wearing and the minor necessaries for the next twenty-four hours: tooth-paste, a toothbrush, deodorant, etc. Everything else could be disposed of. The clothes were mainly dirty, as he had not been able to do any washing for a week, so he threw them in the waste bin under the desk. The rest he packed into the suitcase. The computer and scanner he put back in their boxes, having pressed the 'reset' button on the computer to carry out an operation the manual described as 'restoring factory settings' which he understood would wipe the hard drive. He put the computer equipment and his suitcase on the desk with a note addressed to the maid, thanking her for looking after the room while he had been staying there, and telling her that what he had left was no longer any use to him, so he was leaving it all to her, to do with as she saw fit. That done, his preparations were complete.

The time of waiting felt as though it would never end. But eventually daylight faded to night, and the digital clock below the television screen was approaching 11:30 p.m. – time for the next step.

John pulled his mobile phone out of the jacket pocket and dialled the number he had been given by the girl at the Novice Airlines desk. It rang three times before being answered by a bright and breezy young thing whose enthusiasm and commitment to customer service could not be faulted, even in the middle of the night.

'I have a booking for the flight to Caracas tomorrow, just after noon, and I have to change the name of the person travelling,' he told her.

'Could I have your booking reference number, please?'

John read it out.

'Just retrieving your details, sir. Ah yes, there's a note here that you might need to make a change. What's the name of the person who'll be travelling?'

'John Biddle.'

She asked for his passport number and he read it out. Then he could hear her tapping away on her computer keyboard.

'OK,' she said 'that change has been made. Now it's done, you won't be able to change it again because you're limited to one change only. You can collect your ticket from the customer service desk inside the terminal building any time from now onwards. Is there anything else I can help you with tonight?'

'No thanks.'

' OK. Have a nice flight.'

John ended the call and made another. The phone barely rang before it was answered.

'Adrian, it's John. It's tomorrow, Tuesday; nine o'clock in the morning. It starts at Bridges Junction. Be there with the money – and come alone.'

'Nine a.m.,' Wright repeated. 'At Bridges Junction. Then what?'

'Then I'll tell you what, Adrian, when I want you to know. Just be there with the money, in a canvas holdall, so it's easy to carry.'

John ended the call before Wright could reply. Then he put the phone on the bedside table, turned off the light, lay down on the bed and tried to sleep.

15

Week Four: Day Two – The Last Day

John woke up. He had managed to sleep though not for very long. He cancelled the alarm he had set, got out of bed and got dressed. He did not go down to breakfast because he knew he would not be able to eat anything. He checked the pockets of the jacket again, then turned on the television, to the morning news programme, and waited for the travel bulletin on the local news section, to make sure that the trains were running to schedule. Part of him was half-hoping that they would not be, so that he would not have to go through with this stupid thing he had dreamed up, this absurd escapade that could only end in disaster. The doubting voice faded away as the ribbon-text along the bottom of the screen announced there were 'no major delays reported' on the trains, and John realised that no obstacles stood in his way. He took one last look around the room, then slipped out into the corridor and closed the door. In reception he posted his room key through the appointed slot in the unattended desk and left.

The walk to the station remained imprinted on his memory. It was the last time he would make such a journey; that part of his life was over. At the corner where he turned off the main road he stopped to drop the envelope addressed to Stephen Dent into the post box, then headed down between the neat rows of bungalows towards the railway line; and the world around him began to grow quiet. Each step took him further away from the roar of the traffic and deeper into the peaceful world ahead of him, where nothing and nobody seemed to be moving. At The Boltons station it was the same: the morning rush was over and there was nobody around; the next train was some way off yet. John walked up onto the platform, to the short row of steel bike lockers. He took out the key of the one he had had on 'hire' for the last few days, put the bag with the book and other items inside and locked it.

He looked at his watch and made sure that his mobile phone was turned on, had a good battery level and a strong signal. He pulled out the gloves and slipped them on. He wondered what Adrian Wright was doing at that moment: waiting, probably, as he was: feeling nervous, as he was. The last few minutes ticked away and John made ready to start. He checked the electronic departure board above the platform, noting that the next two trains due to arrive there were running on time – he needed them to. John's train was on its way to The Boltons from the airport and Wright's was about to arrive at Bridges Junction. Time to call Adrian.

'Adrian, good morning. It's John.'

' Listen, there's a problem. We couldn't get the mon . . . '

'No, there isn't. Don't lie to me, Adrian. Do as you're told. You're short of time. There's a train approaching platform two, heading north. Get on it.'

'Where am I going?' Wright asked, trying to get the information to give to those who would be shadowing him.

'I'll tell you when it's time to get off. Just make sure you get on.' John terminated the call and turned his phone off. His own train was approaching.

He boarded it, sat down and tried to keep calm, all the way up the line to North Downham, where got off. He found an inconspicuous place to stand – his back to the wall at the side of the kiosk on the platform, behind a group of grey panthers – turned his phone on again and waited. Time passed.

'The next train to arrive at platform two will be the South Coast Regional Trains service to London River Crossing, calling at South Suburbia and London River Crossing. Customers for London's Elizabeth the Second station should join this train and change at South Suburbia. This is the service from Asham.'

It was also Wright's train.

John peered out from behind the kiosk, waiting for his first sight of the approaching train. As it appeared he dialled again.

'Get off the train and cross to the down platform through the underpass,' John told Wright, 'and get on the next train going south.' He turned the phone off again, reached into his pocket and turned on the mobile phone jammer.

Moments later Wright's train rolled into the station and stopped. The doors opened and people began disembarking. Several of them were looking in a confused way at their mobile phones, which suddenly seemed to have stopped working mid-call, leaving them at a complete loss. Wright Arse was a little way along the platform, dressed as he had been when John had first seen him, and carrying the canvas holdall that John had told him to bring the money in. John fell in behind the group of passengers making their way down into the underpass. Most would leave the station at its far end, a few, like himself and Wright, were making their way to the southbound platform. John walked slowly, looking out for any of Wright's men, whom he felt sure must be amongst the crowd. Wright did exactly as he was told, walking up the stairs at the far end of the underpass and taking up a position close to the edge of the platform. He grasped the holdall firmly, as though he feared John's plan would be to snatch it from him and make a run for it. John walked away from Wright and stood close to the wall at the back of the platform, trying hard not to stare at his intended prey, or at anyone else he thought might be associated with him. Several minutes later the next train arrived. Both of them got on. The doors slid shut and it pulled smoothly away. John noted which doors the guard was working from, then shut himself in the toilet.

'This is the South Coast Regional Trains service to Asham, calling at all stations to Asham,' the automatic announcement system told them. 'The next station-stop is Lord's Copse. This train will now call at Lord's Copse and all stations to Asham.'

The train headed southwards along the tracks, in the direction that John and Wright had both come from. His plan, he told himself, was going smoothly.

Lord's Copse station came and went. John reached into his jacket pocket and flicked off the mobile phone jammer, pulled out his phone and rang Wright again. Without giving him the time to say a word, John told him to stand between the doors where the guard was stationed. He turned off the phone and flicked the jammer on again. Two carriages away, Wright stood up and walked down the aisle to where the guard was standing, ready to operate the doors on arrival at their next stop.

'The next station-stop on this service will be The Boltons,' declared the disembodied voice. 'The next station-stop is The Boltons.'

This was John's cue to move. He left the sanctuary of the toilet and began walking down the aisle towards Wright, trying to make his arrival behind him coincide with the train's entry to the station. As he got close, Wright glanced sideways but, not recognising him, looked away again. John made as if to pass behind him on his way further down the aisle, so Wright had to step forward, towards the guard, who was making ready to open the doors of the decelerating train.

John stepped forward behind Wright and pressed the nozzle of the replica gun, hidden in his jacket pocket, into the small of his back. Wright stiffened.

'Stay still until I tell you to move,' John told him quietly. 'And if you don't do exactly as I tell you, well, you can guess what's going to happen.'

Wright started to speak, but John told him to shut up, jabbing the gun even more firmly into his back. Wright did as he was told. The train slowed down and came to a stop. The guard turned his key to release the doors, and stepped down onto the platform.

'Step forward,' John told Wright, and prodded him again with the gun. The first heart-stopping moment was approaching, the first place where his plans could go disastrously wrong.

The guard looked left and right along the length of his train, to make sure no passengers were still getting on or off. In what seemed, to John, like slow motion, he got back onto the train, reached up to the buttons on the control panel in the door surround, and pressed the first button, to close and lock all the doors except his, which remained open. John's muscles tensed. The guard pressed the second button on the panel. There was a hiss of released compressed air and the doors in front of him began to move. John pushed hard on Wright's back, propelling him forward through the narrowing gap onto the platform and quickly followed just before the doors snapped shut. The bemused guard merely pressed the button which gave the signal to the driver for the train to depart, shaking his head at the stupid antics of two grown men who should have known better.

With one eye on Wright, and the gun still pressed firmly into the small of his back, John saw the train slide away from the platform, several angry-looking faces pressed up against the windows of its doors: Wright's shadows, he thought, now out of the picture – for the time-being at least.

'Over the footbridge to the other platform,' John told Wright, tersely, 'and let's do it quickly. We don't have much time.'

One behind the other, they marched over the footbridge and down the steps onto the 'up' platform. There was only just enough time for John to get to the cycle locker and retrieve the bag that held his part of the exchange, before the northbound train which formed the next part of his plan arrived. Catching this train was crucial because it had left the airport station moments before the train he and Wright had just got off would arrive there, so any agents of Arse marooned on the one heading south would not have arrived in time to catch this northbound train. They got on and the doors closed behind them.

'Go to the toilet compartment,' John commanded. 'The disabled one at the end of the next carriage.' The train, like the station they had just left, was almost deserted. John had chosen well.

Once inside the toilet compartment John told Wright to press the buttons, mounted on the far wall, that first closed and then locked the electrically-operated sliding door. Wright did as he was told. When he turned back to face his captor, he found that John had pulled the gun out of his pocket so it was in plain view, to stamp his authority on the situation. With the other hand, he reached into his jacket pocket and turned on the GPS jammer.

'You'll never get away with this, Biddle,' Wright said. 'Armed robbery is a serious crime.'

'I've got no intention of committing a robbery,' John told him. 'I've come to make the exchange we agreed on, and this . . .', waving the gun in front of Wright, 'is merely my insurance policy, to make sure you stick to your part of the bargain.'

Wright looked unsure.

'Well, if you really have come to make the exchange, can

we get it over with?' he said, a hint of fear audible in his voice.

'Show me the money,' John demanded.

Wright bent down slowly, opened the zip on the bag he was carrying, pulled the top of it apart and let John look inside. It was full, John could see, of bundles of money: the used fifty-pound notes he had said he wanted. Wright made a lunge for the gun, while he thought John's guard was down, but John saw him coming. He whipped it away just in time, leaving the Arse man's fingers clutching at air. John's anger and frustration got the better of him and he brought the butt of the gun down sharply on the side of Wright's head. Wright gave a startled yelp and moved away, to cower in the corner. John was back in control. Grabbing the handles of the holdall, he dragged it towards him.

'This is what you came here for,' he said, pulling The Book of Excuses out of his bag. 'And there's a little something else for you to think about when you get a spare moment. It's a disc I made, by scanning the pages of your precious book onto a computer. It also contains copies of other documents that can be used to prove what you and Perma-way have been up to. And there's more than one copy; there are three. One is coming with me; I've sent one to our friend Stephen Dent; and the third is on its way to a solicitor, with a letter, instructing him to release it to the press through Cliff Maxford, or anyone else who wants a newsworthy story, if he doesn't hear from me at regular intervals from now into the foreseeable future. I've also recorded a confession of my 'crime' on it, of stealing The Book and a file of papers that identifies Roamer-Phone as 'RP' in the Perma-way spreadsheet. And I've named you and the Perma-way directors as the men responsible for this scam so even if, eventually, the accusation doesn't stick, life will be pretty uncomfortable for all of you for quite a long time. You know how long these fraud trials can last. And my solicitor won't hear from me if anything happens to me, or if you and Perma-way don't pay for my silence on a regular basis.'

'But you've just been paid,' Wright exclaimed. 'One million in Sterling, in untraceable notes – what you asked for.'

'Yes, but now I'm being greedy,' John replied, 'and I'm telling you that I want more – five thousand more, in fact – each and every month, paid into a Swiss bank account. I'll phone and give you details when I'm ready. You and your Perma-way chums shouldn't have a problem with that. Greed's something you understand very well.'

'You won't get away with it,' Wright growled. 'You *can't* get away, and there's nowhere to hide.'

'I shall get away. Take your clothes off and give them to me.'

'Take my clothes off!' Wright exploded. 'What the hell for? Are you a pervert as well as a criminal?'

'Do I have to shoot you, or will hitting you again be enough?' John asked, raising the gun.

Wright whimpered and started to undress. His naked body was not a pretty sight. John put The Book of Excuses on the edge of the wash-basin.

'Put these on,' he instructed, pulling the pink leather bondage gear he had bought in Fetishica out of the bag.

Wright stared at him in defiance and disbelief. He opened his mouth to protest, but John hit him again – not hard, though hard enough for Wright, who, when it came to violence against his person, was a coward. In under a minute he was dressed in the pink leather thong and bodice and looking like a withered old pole-dancer. Now came the difficult part.

'Turn around, and grab the rail,' John said, indicating one of the bars attached to the wall to help disabled people.

Wright, still frightened of being hit again, did as he was told after only a moment's hesitation, during which time John started to raise the gun again. The handcuffs John put on Wright fitted perfectly, as did the pink leather gag he applied once his captive was securely fastened to the grab-rail. Now he really looked a complete arse – in every sense of the word. John put the gun on the floor, collected the discarded clothes and stuffed them into the bag which had held The Book. Reaching past Wright, who was now whimpering quietly through the gag, John pressed the button on the wall to unlock and open the door. When it had slid fully open he backed out, both bags clutched in one hand, while he pressed the 'close' button of the door. Quickly, he reached into his jacket pocket and extracted the smoke cartridge. He pulled out its locking pin with his teeth and hurled it through the narrowing gap just as the door closed. Then he took the key he had stolen from the train guard a few days before, and locked the door.

Hurrying away from the toilet, he walked swiftly forward through the length of the carriage ahead and into the next one. He walked on until he reached the front set of doors, and stood alongside them on the right-hand side of the train, as though waiting to get off at the next station, which was Lord's Copse, and could not be far away now. As the train began to slow down, ready to make its stop, he became suddenly very nervous. He was about to attempt the most dangerous part of his plan. There were a number of ways in which it could go wrong, and if it did, he had no alternative.

The train came to a halt at Lord's Copse, but the doors refused to open – as he knew they would. He had discovered from his reading of The Book of Excuses, that these new trains relied on receiving a GPS signal to identify their location so that only the right sets of doors would open at stations which short platforms. The book had told him that if that signal were lost, none of the doors would open automatically for safety reasons; that was the situation he had hoped to create by activating the GPS jammer, and he had succeeded. Now the train would stay in the station while the driver and guard tried to fix the problem, which they would not be able to do because they would not discover what had caused it in the first place. He also needed to distract attention from himself and what he was about to do, which is where the smoke canister, the locked toilet door and Adrian Wright, the involuntary old pole-dancer, came into the picture. Even as the guard was struggling to understand why the door controls refused to respond, the driver would hear an alarm inside his cab telling him one of the smoke detectors had been triggered. When the train crew went to investigate, which they would have to do before they could move off again, they would be further delayed by the locked toilet door. When they managed to work that one out, God only knew what they would think of what they found inside. Sadly, John would never find out, as by then he would be gone – or he would be if his plan went smoothly.

The guard stabbed furiously at the button that should have unlocked the doors of his stationary train. Then he heard the driver's voice over the speakers of the public address system.

'This is a staff announcement: would the conductor contact the driver, please? Conductor to contact the driver, please.'

'Hi, Tom. Fred here,' said the guard, pressing the intercom button. 'What's up?'

'We've got a smoke detector triggered in the disabled toilet in car two. Can you go have a look? And have you got a problem with the doors?'

'Yes and yes. The doors won't unlock, but I'll do the toilet check first. Can you tell the punters?'

'OK.'

The guard took his keys out of the control panel and walked away up the train towards the toilet. It was turning out to be one of those days – and this, he thought, was only the first run on the shift. What else could go wrong, he wondered, before the day was out?

John stood by the doors, waiting; time was running out. On the public address system, the driver had just announced 'a delay in opening the doors due to a technical fault, which the train crew are attempting to rectify'. Through the glass panels in the doors between the carriages, John saw the guard arrive at the toilet and bang on the door to see if there was anyone inside. He got no answer, but the door was clearly locked, so he knocked again.

John started to sweat; by now he should have been gone.

Receiving no reply, the guard decided to open the toilet from the outside with his master key. As the door slid back, a cloud of smoke billowed out into the end of the carriage.

'What the hell?' the guard exclaimed, taking a step back and coughing.

John started to get desperate. If he did not get away soon, there was a grave risk that he might be caught, as Wright, if he got himself free, identified him. It had to come soon, or his chance would be lost. But where was it? Where was it?

The smoke in the toilet was beginning to clear, allowing the guard to make out a grotesque pink shape in the corner. It gradually revealed itself as a woman – or was it a woman? – dressed like a stripper, handcuffed to one of the bars on the back wall of the cubicle. Until then, being a man of the world, he thought he had seen everything. Now he realised the world was a far, far stranger place than he had ever imagined it to be, and began to wonder whether he had really seen much of life at all. Then he started thinking, and decided that this thing, this person, would not have handcuffed itself to the wall – there must have been someone else to do it for them. He heard a train arrive alongside his on the down tracks and stop, but he paid no attention to it because he was deep in thought, realising that this was one of the two men he had seen getting on the train at The Boltons. He thought they had been acting strangely, walking very close together. But where had the other one gone? Leaving the man in pink still trapped in the toilet, he began to walk forward to the front of the train, because he knew for sure that the one he was looking for was not behind him, in the back section. As he walked, the train beside them gave a snort of compressed air; a door closed and it started to move. The guard stepped through the sliding doors between the carriages and stared into the front one, behind the driver's cab. There was no-one there: it was empty. In the driver's cab, another warning light had started to flash.

John locked himself in the toilet compartment in the deserted carriage of the old, slam-door train heading south, away from Lord's Copse station. He was exhilarated. He breathed huge sighs of relief. It had worked. He had got away with it completely unseen and was now on his way to the airport. Wright was trapped on the stationary train at Lord's Copse. His cronies would all be trapped on another stationary train, stuck behind Wright's, somewhere between the airport and Lord's Copse on their way north from the airport, in pursuit of their boss and his captor. None of the northbound trains could move, and Wright could not phone anyone, even if he were free, because the GPS and phone jammers were now nestling safely out of sight in the bottom of the waste bin on the northbound train right where John had been standing until the southbound train had come to a stop alongside it.

That train had arrived not a moment too soon for John, because it had begun to look as though he might be caught, the guard having jumped to the right conclusion far more quickly than John had allowed for, particularly as his means of escape was running late. His fingers were itching to get on with it as the other train arrived; it seemed to take an age to slow down and come to a halt. The two jamming devices were in the bin; the two bags were in his right hand and he was ready to act with his left. With frantic glances back down the carriage he waited . . . and waited . . . and waited – or so it felt to him. It was imperative that he did this without being seen, because no-one must know where he had gone. Simply getting off was not an option, because he would certainly have been spotted on camera and might well have been apprehended as soon as he set foot on the platform at the airport. This way, his escape would be seen only later, when the footage from the train's cameras was viewed, by which time he would, he hoped, be many, many miles away.

Eventually the old, slam-door train on the southbound track had come to a halt. With one last glance down the carriage, John pushed his hand into the recess where he knew the emergency door-release handle was located. He pulled it down. There was a hiss as the compressed air that kept the doors closed was released. He pushed the doors apart and reached out across the divide between the two trains to grab at the nearest door handle on the other side. He pulled the door open. His heart was in his mouth as he launched himself across the void between the trains into the southbound one and shut the door behind him. The doors on the northbound train slid slowly shut, moved by the residual air pressure in their cylinders, closing themselves an instant before the guard entered the far end of the carriage looking for the 'other man'.

The northbound trains may well have been delayed by John's antics that day, but those heading south were not, including the one John was travelling on, so it was not long before it arrived at High Weald International Airport station. John got off, his appearance altered by his having reversed his jacket. He carried only the bag containing the money; the one with Wright's clothes and the stolen guard's keys he had stuffed into the waste-bin in the toilet compartment he had just left. The public face of Roamer-Phone leered down across the platforms. John could not resist grinning at it as he passed.

Going somewhere? You bet your life I am! he thought. I wonder which of us has earned the most from your lords and masters in the last few hours. Still you, I should think. Oh well, no-one promised that life would be fair.

He walked briskly along the platform, up the stairs, across the footbridge, along the elevated walkway over the bus stands and into the airport terminal building. Once inside, he went straight to the Novice Airlines customer service desk, hoping there would not be a queue. He was in luck. The girl behind the counter looked up and smiled.

'Good morning, sir. Welcome to the Customer Service Ticket Sales Desk of Novice Airlines, the airline that serves you with sunshine and smiles. My name is Karen.' It said so on the huge and luminous name badge she wore. 'How may I help you today?'

'My name is John Biddle, You're holding a ticket for me, for the Caracas flight.'

'John Biddle,' she echoed, turning away to consult her computer screen.

Seconds passed, turning into minutes, as the computer searched its memory for his name. John glanced over his shoulder anxiously, fearing that every second might bring pursuit closer.

'As yes,' she said, at last. 'May I see your passport, please?'

John handed it over. She opened it and looked at his photograph, looked up at him, then back down again.

'It's the beard,' John said. 'It's a recent addition. I'm not sure it works.'

'It's fine, sir,' she smiled. 'And so is the ticket.' She unlocked a filing cabinet behind her, pulled open one of the drawers and, turning back, slid his ticket and passport towards him across the counter. 'Your check-in is at the

Super Class desk, just at the head of the aisle to your left. It's open now so you can go straight there. Have a nice flight.'

' Thank you,' John replied with a smile of relief. 'I rather think I'm going to.'

He made his way to the check-in desk, where the ticket was converted into a boarding pass by a girl called Katie who was a clone of Karen.

'Forgive me for asking,' John said, 'but are you and Karen, on the ticket desk, sisters?'

She smiled sweetly and said, 'No, sir, we're not even related. It must be the uniforms; they tend to make us all look alike.'

Instead of going straight to passport control, John went to the bank of left-luggage lockers, where the rats were waiting for him. His nerves were jangling again as he approached the final hurdle, where there were risks he could not easily control and where everything he had achieved, having come so far, could all be snatched away from him and he could find himself going away, not to South America, but to prison instead. When he opened the door, he was greeted by a strong smell of rat.

There's no gain without pain, he thought. He opened the small suitcase he had put on the bottom shelf and carefully lowered the rats' cage into it. Shutting the case securely, he pulled it out and closed the locker door. Then he made his way to the men's toilet at the far end of the check-in hall, carrying the suitcase and the bag with the money in it, and locked himself in one of the cubicles. Here he took out the rats' cage and stood it on the floor. He opened the holdall, took out the money, bundle by bundle, and packed it carefully into the suitcase: it fitted perfectly. He took the last computer disc out of his jacket pocket and laid it on top of the notes with his mobile phone alongside. He shut the suitcase and locked it, he picked up the cage and perched it on top. Next he slipped off the jacket he was wearing and hung it up on the back of the door. Slowly and carefully, he opened the door of the cage and, with his still-gloved right hand, pulled the rats out one at a time and dropped each into a pocket of the jacket, then zipped the pockets. He slipped the empty cage into the holdall, pulled his gloves off and dropped them in too. Draping the jacket over his arm, and hoping that its movement against his hip and thigh as he walked would disguise the presence of the rats, he left the cubicle and the toilet, pushing the holdall into the waste basket as he went. If it caused a bomb-scare later that might further help to cover his tracks by creating an added diversion.

From the toilet, John made his way to passport control. He joined the end of the shortest queue and waited, his nerves jangling and a sickly feeling invading his stomach. The passport officer took a long, hard look at his face and the photograph, then shut the passport and gave it back with a curt nod. John walked on into the security-checking area, going as slowly as he could, looking for a machine operated by a woman – praying that there was a machine being operated by a woman that day. There was, and he joined the queue.

As John moved closer to the front of it, it seemed that the raucous clanging of a fire bell grew louder and louder in his head. It won't work. It will work. It can't work. It has to work. It was the jangling of his nerves.

Then he reached the head of the queue. He pretended to fiddle around with his jacket while he surreptitiously slid open the zips on the pockets. Then he placed it in the plastic tray, praying as hard as he could that his plan would work. The tray went on the belt and began to move towards the opening in the end of the scanner. He quickly put the suitcase on the belt as close as he could to the back edge of the tray. They went in together, and he held his breath while he walked through the archway that was the metal detector. What came next was not a heavy hand, landing on his shoulder to signal that it was all over, but a scream from the woman on the X-ray scanning machine. She had been working for some hours by then, watching images of passengers' coats, bags and other possessions sliding smoothly across the screen as she searched for the illegal or suspicious objects she had been trained to spot. What had shocked her out of her passivity was an image of the animated skeletons of two rats, now free of the confines of John's jacket pockets and running about on the belt and across the top of his case. She screamed again and pushed herself and her chair violently away from the machine. Everyone swung round to stare at her, except John, who stepped forward as his jacket, one of the rats and his case emerged from the end of the scanner. Grabbing the case, he slipped away into the crowd before anyone in officialdom realised he had done so.

He walked quickly through the crowded departure lounge, experiencing a soaring feeling of euphoria, as his stress and anxiety slipped away from him. He found it hard to believe he had achieved what he had set out to do. Now all that was left was to get to the gate, where the flight was already boarding, and find out whether Angela was there. At that thought his doubts sprang up again, and he started to hurry.

He ran down the steps into the departure lounge, where the last few passengers were just filing past the girls doing the boarding checks. He showed one of them his boarding card and passport, and was waved through. Then he was in the narrow corridor that was the air-bridge, leading to the door of the huge machine that was about to cast off its earthly bonds and take him, and the money – and Angela, if she was there – across the Atlantic to a new life on a far and distant shore. He passed through the doorway, the last passenger to board, and was directed to his seat, next to the one person he now knew would make all this worthwhile. She looked pale, anxious and confused for she did not recognise the man with the beard who sat down beside her and stared at her so keenly.

'Angela,' he said, 'it's me, John I made it.'

Her face broke into a beaming smile and she threw her arms around him.

'You came,' she said. 'You really came.'

Fifteen minutes later the plane was airborne, its four massive jets thrusting it upwards into the clear blue of the sky heading west, towards the Atlantic, towards the New World and their new life together. John and Angela sat side by side in companionable silence, holding hands, having toasted each other in the airline's complimentary champagne.

In another ten minutes, with High Weald International Airport slipping further and further away into the distance behind them, the seat-belt sign lights went out and the cabin crew came down the aisles asking if everyone was comfortable and if there was anything they needed.

'Is it possible for me to make a phone call from here?' John asked.

'Yes, sir, of course,' the stewardess said. 'I'll get you the phone.'

She returned a few minutes later with a phone that she plugged into a socket in the arm of his seat.

'Whichever country you're calling, you'll need the international dialling code to start with. If it's the UK it's four-four, then the number you want to call, with the first zero missed off.'

The number John tapped in was one he had memorised as part of his preparation for the day's events: Adrian Wright's mobile. Wright did not answer, and it rang for a long time before the answering service responded. John could only imagine where he was and what he might be going through; he smirked and then laughed out loud.

What sort of story, John wondered, would he have to concoct to explain his presence in the toilet compartment on the broken-down train, in the outfit he was wearing, with a gun on the floor and a spent smoke canister alongside it, and a rather strange book resting on the edge of the washbasin, without incriminating himself and his masters in Perma-way and Roamer-Phone. That's going to keep him busy for some time to come, I think.

The answering service interrupted John's happy thoughts.

'Hello,' John said, after the tone. 'This is John Biddle, calling for Adrian Wright. Adrian, I just wanted to say hello, and let you know I'm fine, and tell you that, well . . . I'm on a plane.'

Epilogue

On Another Day – In Another Week

Young James Crowthorne stood on the station platform at Howards Heath, waiting for his train to arrive, in something of an excited mood, looking forward to his first day in his new job. The opportunity to take up a post as an actuarial assistant at PLGC's head office in South Suburbia had come up suddenly and unexpectedly. It was too good a chance to turn down and he had grabbed at it with both hands. Having to commute was going to be a bit of a pain, but it was something he supposed he would get used to. The job was a good one, and his new boss, Roland Smythe, and the others he had met at his interview had seemed very nice. Admittedly, the trains going to and returning from the interview had both run late, but he had been able to use his mobile phone on both journeys to say he was being delayed. And that was not likely to happen every day, was it?